Hinton

A novel of murder, international intrigue, and oil

Jim Peach

Aakenbaaken & Kent

Hinton

A novel of murder, international intrigue, and oil

This book is a work of fiction. Any similarity of the fictional characters to any actual person is coincidental. Actual persons mentioned in the story are depicted accurately to the best of the author's knowledge.

ISBN: 978-1-958022-14-6

Dedication

For Katie

My truly amazing daughter

Part 1

Places

Someone's gonna get hurt before you're through

Someone's gonna pay for the things you do

Waylon Jennings and Willie Nelson

Chapter 1

Norman, Oklahoma

Millie was always fun. Everyone should have a Millie. No one understood that better than Professor Eddie Hinton. The two old friends had been flirting for many years with carefully proscribed rules that had never been discussed. The rules were simple. This flirtatious quasi-romantic relationship was just between the two of them. No one else would ever know. Nothing was off-limits except propositions or invitations to something more. Sexual innuendos, particularly vague references to some distant but mythical sexual encounters were strongly encouraged. When it started both Hinton and Millie were married but nothing in the rules changed after Hinton's divorce and the death of Millie's husband. Yes, she was an attractive woman, and both were suddenly single but without ever talking about it, it was clear that neither one wanted to spoil their special relationship.

Millie Parker started her career at the University of Oklahoma in the OU Foundation, the money raising arm of the university. In her two years at the foundation, she met and married Billie Joe Parker, a former football player and assistant coach who had become the alumni relations officer in the athletics department. Millie and Billie Joe, who happened to be black, faced innumerable obstacles when they were attempting to buy a house in Norman. Despite the Fair Housing Act and other legislation, no one wanted to sell a house to a mixed-race couple. Each house they looked at was suddenly already under contract or withdrawn from the market. After weeks of frustration in the real estate market,

Millie, with Billie Joe's enthusiastic approval, took Hinton with her to find a house. They soon found an appropriate house on Rosemont Avenue, not far from the university and not far from Hinton's house on Elmwood Drive. They closed on the house in just a few days. Both houses were within walking distance of the university.

Changing jobs from the foundation to the dean's office was a nice promotion in status and salary for Millie. She quickly established herself as indispensable. She was very good at her job. Among other things she was widely known as the fixer, and she seemed to know everyone on campus. Faculty, staff, and students knew that a phone call from Millie could fix most problems. If a faculty member could not get the overhead light in his office repaired, a call or quick visit to Millie would always get it done fast. If a student could not find a faculty member during office hours or get an appointment to discuss some real or imagined grievance, Millie would arrange it. No one, not even Dean Timothy Crowdey, dared to cross her. Millie was the fixer.

Before coming to the university, Millie worked in Dallas for an airline. She took care of problems with the airline's best and wealthiest customers, some of whom even had Millie's cell phone number. If you needed a first-class ticket on a full flight to Paris tomorrow, call Millie and she would get it. She was the fixer. Millie took full advantage of the airline's heavily discounted flights for employees and had visited 23 countries before she left the job. Her goal had been 30 countries by the time she was 30 but sometimes life gets in the way. She was also an accomplished photographer, winning prizes in several exhibitions in Texas and Oklahoma. Friends had often suggested that she quit her job and go professional.

Billie Joe, Millie, and Hinton had a lot in common. All were native Texans living and working in Oklahoma. They never quite figured out

2

whether they were illegal immigrants or just unwelcome guests. They all loved West Texas, especially Brewster County which is home to Big Bend National Park. For different reasons, each felt at home in Alpine, Marfa, Marathon, Terlingua, or the park itself. There is just nothing like a sunrise in that part of the world and everyone you met, at least the locals, always had a story to tell.

And then, there was their collective and individual obsession with country and western music. They could drink beer and play CW trivia for hours. "What was the last song recorded by Hank Williams?" The answer, of course, was "I'll never get out of this world alive." They thought, without debate, that country music said everything there was to say about life, relationships, love and getting up when you have been knocked down. No one needed a psychologist or a marriage counselor. When Hinton's marriage was ending, the first date he had, set up by a friend, was with the soon-to-be ex-wife of their marriage counselor. While this relationship went nowhere, the thought of that brief romance still brings a smile to Hinton's face. Country music and good whiskey are better than any marriage counselor.

Billie and Hinton had become good friends on the handball courts. One day Hinton was looking for someone to play and no one volunteered until Billie said he would defeat the undefeatable. Hinton had been on campus for nearly three years, played handball frequently, and had not been defeated. Once, he had been ranked in the top 100 by the Handball Association of America – an accomplishment that often gave him more satisfaction than being one of the most recognizable figures on campus. Students wanted to be in his classes. Other faculty members sought his advice. Frequently, Hinton thought this was all a joke. How could he possibly be the highly respected Professor Eddie Hinton? In his view of the world, he was still just a kid from West Texas who was happiest drinking a cold beer, eating a good chicken fried steak, and playing pool under the light of the neon moon.

Billie beat Hinton that day. The games were close and lasted a long time. When the last game was over, the two men were exhausted and sat down on the floor leaning against opposite sides of the handball court. Then, with whatever small amount of energy they had left, they started laughing and then talking.

Billie grew up in Fort Stockton, Texas where he was a star running back, wide receiver and occasional defensive back on the high school football team. In most years, the Fort Stockton Panthers were not a very good football team but with Billie they were never out of a game and twice played for the district championship. Football was also Billie's ticket out of West Texas. Billie's family was one of only three or four black families in Fort Stockton, which had a well-deserved reputation as a redneck community. Billie's father was the best electrician in West Texas. If you could get William Parker to install or fix anything electrical, you knew it would be done correctly and that it would last. So, Billie's family was tolerated, if not welcomed, in the area.

Hinton grew up in Junction, Texas not far from Billie's home in Fort Stockton. His parents owned a car repair shop, a laundromat, and a small grocery store in Junction. Hinton was three years older than Billie and more interested in team roping and baseball than football. The two may have met briefly in high school when Hinton's dad hired Billie's father to completely re-wire the car repair shop after a small fire. Billie was not certain of this, and neither was Hinton. The two friends took very different roads to the OU campus. Billie enrolled at Texas Tech, where he was again a star football player, and had a brief pro career. Hinton went to Austin to attend the University of Texas. He was soon cut from the baseball team but discovered economics, languages, and

4

petroleum geology.

Billie and Eddie continued laughing, talking, and playing handball until Billie was killed at the intersection of Chautauqua and Highway 9 by an over-loaded hay truck which failed to stop at the newly installed traffic light.

Millie's call early Friday afternoon came as no surprise to Hinton. She called him often, sometimes just to talk about life, sometimes to talk about sports, and occasionally she called to talk about some burning university issue. Her greeting this time was formal,

"Professor Hinton, the Dean would like to see you at your earliest convenience. Are you available?"

Of course, this meant that the Dean was standing by her desk. Some people just can't make their own phone calls. Although the answer was obvious, Hinton asked Millie when the dean would like to see him. Millie answered without hesitation that he wanted to see him now. Hinton told her that he could be there in five or six minutes, and Millie said that would be quick enough.

The walk from Hinton's office in Memorial Stadium to the Dean's office in Adams Hall only took about two minutes. A window of five or six minutes would give him the chance to make the walk longer with a quick detour through the South Oval. The OU campus looked like a university should look – well-landscaped, beautiful old red brick buildings, and very old large trees. Even a brief walk through campus was always a pleasure. Besides, it would give Hinton a minute or two to ponder the universe and, perhaps, solve the world's problems. Peace in the Middle East would be nice or maybe getting corporate money out of politics. The list was long. Millie and Hinton often joked about solving the world's problems. Hinton always thought that Millie, aka the fixer, had a better chance of solving these problems than he did.

Office space was not plentiful on the OU campus, and Hinton was one of the very few people who had two offices on campus. In addition to academic duties, he had another obscure title. Hinton was the Faculty Athletics Representative (FAR) to the NCAA. All universities that engage in NCAA sports were required to have a FAR. Few people understand what a FAR does. The FAR is supposed to be an independent voice for athletics on campus and can't be paid by the athletics department. The FAR's job description includes providing advice to the university president and the athletic director on all things athletic. Mainly, the FAR is supposed to look out for the welfare of students. Violations of the rules and abuse are high on the list. The NCAA president, Mark Emmert, was fond of saying that the NCAA was all about student-athlete welfare, but everyone understood that the highest priority was money.

FARs often have a travel budget which allows them to go to away games and attend various conference and NCAA conventions. Being a FAR was time consuming but a great deal of fun. Hinton enjoyed getting to know the athletes, coaches, and administrators – something most faculty do not get to do. Being a FAR also meant that you were an insider. Hinton had the cell phone numbers of the president, the athletic director, and most of the coaches. He could go where he wanted. He was given a pass that allowed him to go to any athletic event and go anywhere in the stadium including the sidelines. When they gave him the pass, he was told that it would even get him into the women's locker room, but he never tried that. More important was that being a FAR meant that, until Billie's death, Hinton and Billie could engage in long sometimes philosophical discussions about sports and pretend that it was work.

The walk was far too short. Back to reality. When Hinton entered the Dean's suite, Millie pointed to the conference room. This was not too unusual, but this gesture indicated that the dean was not alone. Hinton was a bit surprised to see only the university president, and a complete stranger who handed him a business card with only a name and a phone number on it. Hinton had seen cards like this before and knew instantly that the stranger worked for the CIA. The Agency, as it was often called, was forbidden by law to operate domestically but maintained numerous offices throughout the country. The offices were small and suitable for only one or two people. The offices were always in nondescript places located in some large office building. If there was a nameplate on the door, it would typically have only the words Law Office or Consultants. There were, of course, no clients, customers, or even a receptionist or secretary. It was highly likely that the name on the card was false. Sometimes the phone number was false as well.

Once or twice, Hinton had been interviewed by one of these anonymous Agency types during an investigation of some nebulous conspiracy. He also knew about these allegedly non-existent agents because he had worked for the CIA for three years after graduating from college. He had been recruited not because of his dual degrees in economics and mathematics, but because he spoke Arabic, French and Urdu. Hinton remembered the final interview well. It was the last of three interviews before he was hired. The first was a telephone interview. The second took place in Dallas at the Hilton Hotel not far from DFW airport. The last interview was a grueling two-day affair that took place at Langley. The so-called interview included thorough physical and psychological exams as well as more traditional interviews with various Agency officials. The odd thing about this process was that he had been told the Agency would reimburse him for expenses.

When it came time to leave, no one said anything about the

7

reimbursement. For a recent college graduate who had not yet found a job, this was a big deal and could have been a serious problem. The young woman who escorted him out of the building asked him about his expenses. Hinton told her $450 for the airplane ticket, $175 per night at the hotel near Dulles Airport, and a few bucks for meals. Without asking for receipts or documentation of any kind, she handed him $975 in cash. Obviously, they had wanted no record that he had ever been there. Hinton did not object.

Several weeks later, Hinton was offered the Agency job. Since he had no other offers, he accepted almost immediately. His three years at the Agency were not boring. Although he was hired as an analyst, he went through training on surveillance, self-defense, and other activities more suited to an agent. It was fun, but Hinton wanted something more. When he told his supervisor that he was resigning to return to graduate school, the supervisor was not exactly pleased but said Hinton would be welcome to return if he wanted. For job references, he was to say that he had worked for the Statistical Analysis Branch of the US Department of Agriculture's Economic Research Service. They gave Hinton a name and a phone number of someone who would vouch for his employment and performance at USDA. There would be nothing to connect him to the Agency and, importantly, in the academic career he was about to pursue, no blight on his record.

President James Henderson opened the conversation.

"Good to see you, Eddie. This gentleman is from a federal government agency, and he needs your help. I am here to assure you that no matter what you decide –help him or not—that you will have my full support. Your university career will not be damaged or compromised in any way. No one will ever know anything about this endeavor. I am also here to tell you that this man really is from a federal agency. He is not a fake. Finally, I want to tell you that I am convinced of the importance of this activity. Mr. Johnston will explain some details. Please ask him any questions you might have."

Chuck Johnston, the stranger with the minimalist business card, began to speak.

"Nothing that I say here is to leave this room whether you agree to do this or not. We have, without your permission, already renewed your security clearance and so you are bound by federal law to keep your mouth shut. Do you understand that?"

"Yes, of course." Hinton replied and Johnston, whose real name was Clayton Delaney, continued.

"How well do you know Professor Douglas Ross?"

Hinton answered honestly but revealed little that was not already widely known. "The history department was recruiting a new faculty member and I mentioned to a friend in the department that they really needed an economic historian. I recommended that they talk to Doug, who had been a classmate in graduate school. His publication record quickly moved him to the top of their list and ultimately the history department hired him even though he was technically an economist."

Johnston nodded then said, "Ross has disappeared. He is not responding to emails, his cell phone is not operable, and no one has seen him on campus for weeks. Three of our analysts have also disappeared. One was our best Libya analyst, the second an expert on the Nigerian economy, and the third one was a key member of our Saudi group. All three are good looking women in their thirties and early forties. All of them met with Ross shortly before they disappeared. One of them was found dead and sexually assaulted in the DC area. The other two are still missing. Both live in London and work in the Embassy. We have reason to think that Ross left the DC area for London shortly after the murder. We think you can find Ross quicker than we can. Are you willing to help out?"

There was no hiding the obvious connection to the oil industry, and Ross had become one of the premier historians of that industry. This was not surprising given that he was distantly related to a former Texas governor and the founder of Humble Oil, Ross Sterling. Oil was a large part of his family history. .

Hinton's response was not exactly enthusiastic.

"Oh shit. I don't think you have the right guy. Doug does not have the *cajones* to attack and kill a woman. He is a dull, plodding historian who is happier examining a stack of corporate documents or drilling records to see if there is something there to provide fodder for his next pedantic journal article. He does enjoy the company of women and at least two of them lived with him for several years. I suspect they left him out of boredom. Really, you don't have the right guy here. There is probably some innocent explanation for Doug's disappearance. In any case, you guys have the resources and know-how to find someone without outside assistance. Besides, I gave up that kind of work when I left the Agency twenty years ago."

Johnston had anticipated this response and was not deterred.

"We think Ross is up to something beyond the disappearance of three women. We don't know exactly what that is, but we are investigating all possibilities. Ross has the knowledge and contacts to be much more than a minor nuisance. Oil markets are always fragile and subject to major disruptions. We want your help to find him and find out if he is part of some larger conspiracy. He is more likely to talk to you than any of us."

Hinton was not impressed. Oil markets are fragile and sometimes price spikes can occur with seemingly minor events. Kidnappings in

Nigeria, a pipeline explosion in Libya, an attack on a Saudi refinery have all been known to cause a price spike. But these events and the subsequent price hikes don't last long. No one can really control the price of oil for a long time. OPEC did this more effectively than most for a while. But it did not last. The simple problem is that there is too much oil in the world and too many players in the game.

Johnston pressed the argument.

"We really need you to help out. We know that you and Ross are scheduled to have dinner at an Indian restaurant in London in ten days. If you could contact him and move the dinner forward a few days, that would be very useful."

Hinton feigned shock and anger, but he was not surprised.

"You bastards have been reading my email. That is the only way you could know about the dinner in London."

Johnston shot back immediately.

"No, in truth, we have only been reading Doug Ross's emails. Your response to him a month ago was an accidental byproduct."

To be honest, Hinton did not care. He had long ago concluded that anything and everything electronic might as well be published in the *New York Times*. Hinton often warned colleagues that anything they put in an email or on social media should be considered public. Someone could and would find it.

The bantering and bargaining continued for some time but ultimately, Hinton agreed to help. Hinton told Johnston that he would need complete details of the missing women, a burner phone, and complete freedom of movement while he tried to locate Ross. Johnston agreed and told him that his first stop would be a day at Langley to be briefed with all the information they had.

President Henderson stayed for the entire meeting. When the

11

meeting ended, he told Hinton to just let him know if there was anything on campus he needed done. He, or Millie, who was to move from the dean's office to the president's office at the end of the month, would take care of it.

Before Johnston left the meeting, he explained that they had taken the liberty of booking a flight for Hinton on Sunday from Oklahoma City to Dulles via Atlanta. The flight information included his trusted traveler number so that he could use the fast TSA lanes at the airport. They had also booked a room for him at the Grand Hyatt near Dulles. When Hinton asked how they got access to his trusted traveler number, Johnston said "With the president's permission, we got Millie to do it." Millie was the fixer.

Chapter 2
Errands

Hinton had a few things to do before leaving for Langley. Not many because he had long ago figured out that the most important travel items were cash, credit cards, and a valid passport. Everything else could be purchased almost anywhere. On the way home he stopped by the bank and withdrew $2,000 in small bills. He would leave some of it for Tanya, Millie's daughter, who had readily agreed to stay at the house and take care of the dog, Fergie.

Fergie had adopted Hinton. Walking home from work one day a couple of years ago, the dog had simply followed Hinton to his house, even though Hinton kept telling the dog to go home. Hinton needed to go to the store. The dog jumped into Hinton's jeep without an invitation and seemed delighted at the prospect of a car ride. Hinton had no intention of keeping the dog, but he did buy a small bag of dog food and a couple of dishes at the store. Later, the dog objected to being left outside and Hinton finally let it in the house.

The next day and for many days after that, Hinton did everything he could to find the dog's owner. The animal shelter said that the dog had no microchip. Hinton could leave the dog there, but it would likely be euthanized. He took the dog home. Tanya put lost-dog posters in all the local veterinarian's offices and throughout the neighborhood. She posted information on social media. Hinton took out an ad in the *Norman Transcript* and did everything he could to find the dog's owner. Nothing worked.

For several weeks, Hinton simply called the animal Dog but realized eventually that Dog needed a real name. He selected Fergie, after Ferguson Jenkins, the great Cubs pitcher. Jenkins pitched 283 complete games in his career but that was not a record at the time. There have been very few complete games by MLB pitchers in the last three decades. The game had moved on but really it still needed the skill, dedication, and perseverance displayed by Fergie Jenkins. Hinton had learned a great deal from Fergie Jenkins. The most important being that institutional loyalty is a one-way street. Individuals can be loyal to the institution, but institutions are not loyal to individuals. After a few bad games, Jenkins was traded from the Cubs to the Texas Rangers. But Jenkins got the last laugh. The next year he had a 25-12 won loss record with the Rangers. If you don't know baseball, that is a very good record. Fergie did not seem to mind the new name and Hinton had become very attached to this dog that no one, not even the vet, could identify as belonging to any particular breed.

Friday evening passed quickly. Hinton thought he needed a barbeque fix before leaving town. Van's on Porter was just what he needed. Van's, a converted gas station, had been there for many years and had been preceded in the same location by Strick's, also a barbeque joint. They had great ribs, greasy fries, and friendly service. Hinton demolished the ribs but skipped the fries. Sadly, they did not serve beer. He said hello to a few friends, went home and tossed some clothes in the washer.

For the most part, Hinton spent Friday evening wondering whether he had made the right decision. He knew that under the best of circumstances he was entering a world of deception and possibly activities that were not exactly legal. Having doubts was not something

14

Hinton engaged in very often. He was a confident, sometimes too confident, man. He had been in some scary places – the dark streets of Calcutta in the middle of the night came to mind instantly—and he knew how to handle himself in dangerous situations. No, it was not potential danger that created the doubts in his mind.

More likely, what was bothering him was whether he was doing the right thing. He did not like the idea of working with the Agency again and the thought of betraying Ross, a colleague, gnawed at his mind. When he left the Agency twenty years ago, he cut all ties. He did not stay in touch with former colleagues. He was determined to become an honest and hard-working academic. The secret game was for someone else to play. He was finished with that. At one point in the evening, he looked at Fergie and said aloud, "Can I change my mind?" Fergie knew that he had said something but offered no useful opinion. The best Hinton could do was to tell himself that he could always back out after being briefed at Langley. He played Patsy Cline music on his tablet. Finally, he fell asleep.

The next morning, he packed a small backpack and a small duffle bag. The packing was easy. A few shirts, underwear and socks, a pair of khakis and an extra pair of blue jeans. Both bags were small enough to be carried on the flight. He needed very little to travel but tossed in a light jacket, electrical converters, and an extra pair of shoes. He had learned the hard way never to buy shoes in the UK. They had peculiar shoe sizes that never seemed right. The Brits must have odd-shaped feet. For some reason, Hinton regretted not being able to pack his Glock-19.

Tanya came by about 10 o'clock. Tanya, named after Tanya Tucker, was Hinton's daughter's best friend. Tanya and Leslie had grown up together. On any given night they might be staying at one house or the other. Leslie had gone off to college at San Diego State University. That was not exactly Hinton's first choice in universities, but Leslie felt comfortable there because it was a favorite vacation spot when she was younger. She liked it. Okay, you might as well choose a place you like to go to college. Most kids don't realize how important that is, but they will live where they go to college for several years. Tanya and Leslie remained good friends and were in touch almost daily.

All too often, Leslie innocently created trouble. On the first day of second grade, the teacher asked each student to describe what their parents did. Leslie responded, "My mom works with computers and my dad is a communist." She did not understand why the teacher was so shocked or why other students laughed. What the hell, "a communist" and "an economist" sound a lot alike. Hinton remembered this incident and many others with great fondness. For now, Tanya would serve as a surrogate daughter.

Fergie, who had eyed the packing with suspicion, was delighted to see Tanya. The dog seemed to understand that he would be well taken care of during Hinton's absence. Who knows what dogs really understand, but there was no denying how pleased Fergie was to see Tanya. Tanya tried without success to refuse the money Hinton gave her. She needed no instructions and she had had a key for many years. She knew the house and what to do. Mainly she came by to reassure Fergie.

Hinton met his ex-wife, Linda, for lunch in Oklahoma City. Despite their divorce or maybe because of it they enjoyed these monthly meetings. A year or so before their marriage ended, Linda had purchased a condo in the City in the Deep Deuce district adjacent to Bricktown, an area that had once been described as a slum, and dangerous at that, had become one of the most attractive and expensive places to live in Oklahoma. Linda could afford it. She was a software consultant who mainly took care of doctors, lawyers, and small businesses. She made a ton of money, and it was true that most of her clients were in Oklahoma City, not Norman. Buying the condo made sense. At first Linda spent three and later four nights a week at the condo and returned to Norman for the rest of the week. Gradually, she spent more and more time at the condo and much less time in Norman.

Hinton knew that their marriage could not survive in this fashion for long. He did not know what to do about it or even if he wanted to do anything about it. One night after dinner, Linda suggested that they should get a divorce. Hinton agreed without hesitation. There were no arguments, no fights. Boredom and neglect ended their marriage. The divorce was as easy as such things can be. Linda kept the condo, Hinton kept the house. After the court proceedings, they checked into the Hotel Skirvin in downtown Oklahoma City. The Skirvin was a great old hotel with a magnificent lobby. It was neutral ground and they had been there before. They made love most of the night. They did not talk about their past together or their future as suddenly liberated individuals. Hinton thought of it as a good-bye gift.

Hinton parked his jeep on 3rd Street near Oklahoma Avenue and only a minute or so from the condo. Linda was on the balcony and said she would be right down. They walked two blocks to La Baguette, a restaurant on 4th Street. Over sandwiches and soup, they did a little catching up on events and people in their lives. Nothing exciting, just small talk. They could not resist sharing a large piece of apple pie. Linda suggested they return to the condo for coffee. A couple of hours later Hinton left for the thirty-minute drive back to Norman. Maybe there is nothing better than sex with your ex. No talking, no commitments, just raw enthusiastic sex.

Hinton also had a dinner date with Millie that evening. Date is probably the wrong word. They simply had dinner together every two or three weeks. Even though they lived about one minute apart, Millie said she had a few errands to run and would meet him at Victoria's on campus corner at 7. Victoria's was an Italian restaurant, always busy, always noisy but they made their own pasta, and everything was very fresh. Millie was already seated when Hinton arrived five minutes early. The first words out of her mouth after Hinton sat down were:

"You got laid this afternoon. Congratulations. How is Linda?"

Was it that obvious? Did it show on his face or in his gestures? Did he have it tattooed on his forehead? Maybe, just maybe, Millie was guessing.

Millie ordered a lasagna roll – something very close to an Italian burrito or rolled enchilada. Hinton ordered his favorite dish, fettuccini Alfredo with sun-dried tomatoes. Both had a glass of Chianti. Then Millie surprised him again.

"Okay, so the strange looking guy with the president was some sort of government agent. You are leaving for London early, and your job is to find Doug Ross. Am I about right?"

Millie had not been in the meeting and Hinton was certain that neither Henderson nor Johnston had talked. How in hell does she figure this stuff out? Millie always had the knack of putting together seemingly unrelated facts to reach a less than obvious conclusion. Millie told him that she had already looked at his calendar and canceled three appointments, two on campus and one with the dentist. She would take care of anything else that came up while he was gone. Millie was the fixer. She was not finished surprising him.

Chapter 3

Langley

Hinton did not enjoy flying. Like millions of others, he found the long lines, crowded waiting areas, mediocre and sometimes unfriendly service, full flights, and cramped seats to be disgusting. He had developed a 700-mile rule. Any trip of less than 700 miles, he would drive instead of fly. Maybe, he thought, this flight won't be so bad. Who wants to get up early enough to catch a 6 am flight?

Hinton arrived at Will Rogers Airport early. It was a small airport and that was a good thing. Hinton was pleasantly surprised at the Delta check-in counter. His ticket was for a first-class seat which meant more legroom, decent coffee and snacks, and not waiting to leave the plane when it arrived. Hinton went through the TSA line in about 30 seconds and searched for a cup of coffee. There were few choices that early in the morning, but he finally found a cup of lukewarm tasteless coffee and a sweet roll. Oh well, he was flying first class. He boarded the flight early and was comfortably seated when he saw a familiar face walk down the aisle towards the rear of the plane. He had a huge smile on his face that he could not hide as Dean Crowley headed for the cheap seats.

The flight to Atlanta was smooth and on-time. Miracles do happen. Hinton did not like Atlanta's Hartsfield-Jackson Airport. Yes, they had spent a lot of money on improvements the last few years, but this could not overcome the fact that the place was too large and there were always too damn many people trying to go from one gate to another. Many of them looked lost and confused. This time, it was different. The gate for his connecting flight to Dulles was only three gates away and in between was the VIP lounge, which he could enter as a first-class passenger. He was tempted by the offer of a bloody Mary from the bartender in the lounge, but years of air travel had convinced him not to drink on flights or the interregnums. He would be in DC soon enough and he had a lot to think about.

What was he getting himself into? Would he be able to do something constructive and useful or was he going down the dark path of betraying an innocent colleague? There was no way to answer these questions on Sunday morning in the VIP lounge at Hartsfield-Jackson. Weighing even more heavily on his mind was Millie. For the first time, he had been thinking of a different kind of relationship with Millie. He wondered if Millie would even consider a romantic relationship. Could he deal with the complications that a serious relationship with an old friend would inevitably bring? Could he deal with telling his daughter Leslie or Millie's daughter Tanya? How would they react? How would Linda react? He and Linda had been close to Millie and Billie Joe.

The flight to Dulles was only a few minutes late. As he boarded the flight, Hinton looked around to see if there were any familiar faces. There were not and he seemed to have lost Dean Crowley in Atlanta. The flight to Dulles was uneventful but as usual it took what seemed like a long time to exit the plane onto the peculiar shuttles at Dulles, go through the terminal and cross the street to the Hyatt.

What Hinton really wanted to do was to go to a baseball game. His Cubs were playing the Nationals and he had only been to the Nationals stadium once. By the time he managed to check into the hotel, the game was already in the third inning and by the time he could get there it would be the fifth or sixth inning. No, he would complete his homework as he should.

Hinton wanted to see the place where the dead analyst had been found. From what Johnston had said, the body of the dead analyst had been found inside the district. This made the task much easier. There were only three or four days in which this could have happened. A quick search of DC's on-line crime reports data base indicated that there were two women murdered during those days. One of the women was a 70-year-old grandmother who had apparently been murdered by her son.

The other victim's name was listed as PN—pending notification—but there was an address, 3724 Windom Pace, NW. Hinton took the shuttle bus from the hotel to the nearest metro station. Were they ever going to finish the metro line to Dulles? The airport was built more than fifty years ago in what had once been beautiful Virginia countryside. The area around the airport was now a thriving urban metropolis in its own right, but still no rail service. Hinton got off the metro at Tenleytown and walked the six blocks to the address on Windom Place. The neighborhood was pleasant with houses that had once been modest, middle-class homes. Now, those houses, like everything else in the district, were expensive. He could probably not afford to live there.

The house shared a common wall with the house next door. Parking on the street in front of the house was prohibited. Hinton walked to the end of the block and up the alley. There was parking in the rear, but it would be difficult to get to the rear door of the basement from the parking space while carrying a body and not be seen. Hinton had the information he needed. It was unlikely that the analyst had been killed elsewhere. If Ross had committed this crime, he was probably invited into the house. Very strange.

He walked to the front for one more look and was surprised to see movement inside the house, probably two people. This was puzzling.

Who could be there? A relative? The killer or killers? Hinton had no clue.

Hinton walked around the neighborhood a bit more and nothing changed his initial assessment that this was probably a low crime area. It was possible but unlikely that this was just a random act. Hinton had learned long ago to do his best to keep an open mind in any investigation –academic or otherwise. He walked back to Tenleytown station to wait for the all too infrequent trains on a Sunday afternoon. After a minute or two he noticed what he thought was a familiar face. Hinton was almost certain he had seen the same woman in the lobby of the Hyatt. Hinton discounted the possibility that he was being followed. Only the Agency knew that he was in the DC area, and they would never be clumsy enough to let him identify a shadow so easily. He was probably imagining things. Still, the woman took the same train and got off at the last stop before Dulles. She also took the shuttle to the airport, but instead of crossing the street to the Hyatt she entered the airport lobby.

In his room, Hinton checked to see if his room had been searched but he didn't think that anything had been disturbed. He looked at his phone to find the score of the Cubs-Nationals game and wished that he had not. The Cubs lost badly, and he had concluded that this was not to be a repeat of the magical 2016 season when the Cubs won the World Series for the first time in 108 years. There would be no excuse for another late October visit to Chicago. Hinton liked the room. It was high enough up to have a great view of airplanes taking off and landing.

A short while later, Hinton went downstairs to eat in the hotel restaurant. There she was again and there was no point in ignoring the fact that he recognized her. They had been seated facing each other only two tables apart. Unavoidably, their eyes met, and he simply smiled at her. They did not speak. Hinton ordered crab cakes and a glass of chardonnay. Her order arrived first and to his surprise it was exactly what he had ordered. Hinton held up his glass and toasted her from a distance. They had no other contact.

After dinner, Hinton went for a walk. The best place to walk was in the airport. According to the app on his phone he walked two miles. Once back in the hotel lobby he found a comfortable chair out of the way of the usual hotel traffic and called Millie. Their conversation did not last long. Millie was trying to clean and do laundry, but she did tell him that Ross had not responded to her email and Hinton knew that if he was being followed then his phone calls were more than likely being monitored.

On Monday morning Hinton checked out of the hotel and left his bags with the concierge. As instructed, he was standing outside the hotel when his ride to Langley arrived. Hinton had never met the driver, but the young man knew how to identify him. The driver explained that Hinton would be briefed by the Deputy Director, David Dubinski. The driver was impressed. Very few visitors were briefed by the DD. Hinton was not impressed. He had not seen David in more than twenty years. They had been hired by the Agency at the same time and went through many of the same training sessions together. David was widely known as Deuce, because when it was his turn to deal in the Thursday night poker games, he always called for deuces wild.

After a minute or two of inconsequential light talk about old times, Deuce got to the point, explaining that this was a high priority effort.

"The director would be here to join in but right now she is at the White House and then will testify before an unscheduled meeting of the Senate Intel Committee. She will explain why we consider this to be so important. For now, it is enough for you to know that the Agency, like DOD, has concluded that the greatest national security threat is climate

23

change. Right now, I will explain why we think Ross is involved in the death of one analyst and the disappearance of two others. We think you can find Ross quicker than we can even though we have several assets involved in the search in DC, London, and elsewhere. We really appreciate the help. The dead analyst's name is Patricia Walker."

Stunned, Hinton interrupted.

"Damn! I knew Patti. We were on several panels together at various energy conferences. She is or was a very bright woman and incredibly knowledgeable about the transportation of oil and LNG. No one knew more about supertankers than Patti. I know she served as assistant secretary in the Department of Energy and that Chevron and Exxon tried to hire her after she left public service. I did not know that she went to work for you. I will miss her."

Deuce continued,

"Yes, you have her bio correct. We know that on the last day of her life, she met Ross late in the afternoon for drinks at the Marriott Hotel in Crystal City. We think they both attended an event at the hotel starting at 5:30. Later, we think Patti and Ross got into her car at the hotel parking garage, but we are not certain. The event was the monthly meeting of the 50-60 Club, a group that celebrates Rock n' Roll music from the fifties and sixties. We are not certain that they were together even though we have the hotel video of the event. Everyone at the event wore a costume. There were several dressed as Buddy Holly, a number who were dressed as Bobby Darin, a few, including Patti dressed as Tina Turner. There were 14 Elvis impersonators, and we think Ross was one of them. Hard to tell."

"We know that Patti was found dead in her NW DC house the next day. She was nude, tied spread-eagled to the bed, and her body was horribly mutilated. It must have been a very painful and lengthy death.

We can show you photos if you want to see them."

Hinton declined and Deuce continued.

"We also know that Ross picked up his rental car from the parking lot at the Wardman Hotel between 10 and 11 that evening and then dropped it off at Dulles, where he boarded a flight to London."

Hinton commented that the Wardman was an expensive place for an academic to stay. He had stayed there once but he was only able to do that with a very hefty conference discount. He liked the place, and it was within walking distance of Patti's house.

Deuce paused and then said,

"We also know that you walked by Patti's house yesterday. Very clever of you to find an address. Did you know it was Patti?"

"I did not know it was Patti's house. I had merely looked up recent murders on the DC crime report database. There was no name for this one. Now, it is my turn for a question. Was the mysterious woman who followed me one of yours?"

Deuce was shocked or so it seemed. "Absolutely not but I will find out who it was. That is very disturbing because only a few people knew you were in DC. As you know, we do not do anything operational in the US. By the way, we identified you from the video cameras installed by the DC police to watch the front and rear of the house. We got the videos indirectly from the FBI. The cameras had been expertly installed. The one in the front of the house was on top of the no parking sign and looked just like the cap on the metal pole holding the sign. The one in the rear was on a transformer on the electric pole. Nice work but we did not do it."

Hinton wanted to know what Patti had been working on. Deuce informed him that her assignment had been a report on the geopolitical implications of transitioning to a carbon free economy within a decade.

25

"As part of her research, she had numerous conversations with political and industry leaders here and abroad. She had also been advising the Saudis to remove Russia as a member of OPEC+. Her reputation and charm provided her with easy access to important people. None of them knew she worked for the Agency. Her cover story was that she worked for a consulting firm. She had a business card with the name and phone number of the company. The phone would be answered –here at Langley if anyone bothered to call. Over several months she informed the Agency that her questions made a few of the industry types and nearly all the politicians nervous. The Agency is open to the possibility that someone other than Ross killed her, but all signs point to Ross."

Deuce then described the two missing analysts. "Cindy Burgess, age 36, was assigned to the economics office in the London Embassy. She is the expert on the region known as MENA."

Hinton, of course, knew that MENA referred to the Middle East and North African Nations.

Deuce continued, "Her specialty is Libya where she lived for three years. Cindy is fluent in Arabic, very well informed about the oil and gas industry, and highly respected. She is everyone's go to analyst on Libya. Cindy was in frequent contact with Patti and was contributing to the transition report. She had dinner with Ross two days after he arrived in London but has not been seen since. The British authorities, including MI5, have been notified and are actively searching for her. Rumor has it that she once had an affair with the German Ambassador to the UK. No one has seen her since the day she had dinner with Ross. Her apartment has been searched."

Deuce continued, "Dianne (Annie) Stoddard, age 33, is a rising star in the world of energy analysts. She usually works here at Langley but has been temporarily assigned to London at the request of the Nigerian

Ambassador, Edward Asiwaju. They had become friends when they were both studying at the London School of Economics. Annie was pleased by the request, and we were happy to accommodate it. Annie had been working with Patti on the transition report. She had lived in Nigeria for a couple of years and had become an expert on the Nigerian oil industry. Over 90 percent of Nigeria's exports are oil. Annie has been staying at a former safe-house near Sloane Square. I could not say this in public, but Annie is a strikingly gorgeous woman—a real traffic stopper. She does her best not to flaunt her looks. She dresses conservatively but it is difficult not to notice her. Annie had dinner with Ross a couple of days after Cindy Burgess disappeared. Like Cindy Burgess, she has not been seen since."

Hinton wanted to ask Deuce what possible motive Ross could have for the disappearance of these two women, but their conversation was cut short when the Agency director, Sally Langford, entered the room. Langford had been hired by the Agency during Hinton's last year. They had met only once when they had chatted briefly during a break in an all-day meeting. Hinton remembered telling Deuce to watch out for her because one day she would be his boss. Hinton did not expect her to remember the conversation. He was wrong. Langford greeted him warmly, as if they were old friends.

The director started talking, "The Agency does not set policy. We gather information and make threat assessments. You probably know from Deuce that our most recent threat assessment listed climate change and potential war in the Middle East as the two most imminent dangers to the US. We are not alone in this assessment. DOD and other intelligence agencies have come to the same conclusion. We are most certain about climate change, but the two threats are related."

"Climate change poses great risks to the nation in terms of rising sea

27

levels, the disruption of agricultural activities, fire danger, and general health of the population. Rising sea levels threaten all our coastal cities. Miami, Charleston, and New Orleans are already using pumps to keep dry. In a few years, coastal residents won't be able to get insurance or mortgages on houses, and banks and insurance companies will be in deep trouble. We could have a recession that makes 2008-2010 look mild by comparison and that is just for starters."

Hinton had known this and more for a long time. He also knew the other side of the story and often had his students write an essay on what the world would have been like without fossil fuels for the last century and a half. Hinton did not interrupt the director.

"There are encouraging signs. BP and Shell have both committed to be carbon net zero within a few years. BP is even installing thousands of EV charging stations in China. Shell and Chevron are investing heavily in wind. The Saudis have invested heavily in Lucid Motors, a potentially serious competitor to Tesla. A German company claims to have a battery for EVs that will allow a range of 1,000 kilometers. A group of mainly European investors called The Institutional Investors Group on Climate Change, who control $40 trillion, will announce in a few weeks that they will no longer invest in any fossil fuels. There are encouraging signs about the development of what amounts to biodegradable plastic. The technology already exists to build housing and commercial buildings that are essentially off the grid. About the only thing the world doesn't have the technology to run without fossil fuels is aircraft. No one has figured out how to fly a plane powered by solar panels, but a Utah company has had some success in battery operated aircraft and hydrogen fuel cells show great promise."

Hinton did not need convincing. He could expand the list. The Director continued, "The Saudis are ready to announce that they will reduce oil output by 1 million barrels per day for five consecutive years and then announce a plan to reduce production further. That is about half of current Saudi production. The Russians who are investing heavily in battery technology are ready to do the same thing. We expect the announcement to be joint. Like the oil companies, the Russians and Saudis are agnostic about where they earn their money, and they seem to have figured out that they don't need oil to be prosperous."

Hinton, who already knew most of this, interrupted. "So where does Ross fit into all of this? Why are these analysts so important to the outcome?"

The Director answered, "A steady move to a carbon free world would be a great thing for everyone on the planet. But sudden changes and announcements would inevitably result in financial market chaos. There are also powerful forces within oil producing nations who oppose any shift away from oil and gas. If Ross is involved, and we think he is, his actions are probably designed to disrupt the process. Either way, we need to know what is going on and of course we want to know what happened to our analysts and why. There is no doubt that oil and gas interests are capable of violence to defend their territory. In the past, they have overthrown governments, carried out assassinations, and spent millions to ensure what they call orderly energy markets. This is the biggest threat to the industry they have ever faced. They will fight it. So we are very grateful that you can help us find Ross."

Hinton knew better than to challenge the director or Deuce, but he was very skeptical. He explained his skepticism,

"Ross is a very unlikely candidate to be a serial killer. He is not a man with physical courage or even a vivid imagination. To do this on his own seems very improbable. If an oil company or some national entity wanted these analysts killed, they would most likely hire a professional assassin if they did not already have one on staff. Why would they turn to an unproven amateur?"

The director was aware of these arguments and explained,

"We have considered the perspective you just described, and we are still open to the possibility that Ross was not involved. Ross had access and opportunity. Under normal circumstances, he would not be on anyone's suspicious persons list, but we also know that there have been three unusually large deposits in his bank account in the last three months. A large payment to Ross just before Patti's murder. Another one was made the day after the murder. So, we ask you to take this seriously."

"Our best guess is that Ross was being paid by the Russians to kill Patti Walker. The signs of a sexual attack were probably staged to cover up the real purpose of the murder. We know that Ross has been to Russia several times. His next book will be on the history of the Russian oil industry. We have tracked the payments to Ross to Dimitri Nogolov, a Russian billionaire who made his fortune in the oil business. Dimitri is also very close to Putin."

Hinton had several questions and started to open his mouth to ask them, but the Director kept on talking.

"From State Department records, we know that Ross has taken at least six trips to Russia in the last four years. We also know that he met with Dimitri Nogolov in Paris and in London on more than one occasion. We know this because Dimitri's chef in his Paris apartment is on our payroll. We do not know exactly what they talked about."

"You might be wondering about Nogolov's motivation, but the answer is simple. Nogolov is part of Putin's inner circle of friends. What Putin wants more than anything is control, influence, and respect on the world stage. There is no secret about that. You can figure that out by reading the press. Putin does not consider climate change to be a serious threat. Putin resents the power that the Saudi's have in oil markets. He doesn't like being the junior member of OPEC. The Russians will do whatever they need to do to be in charge. If they hired Ross to kill Patti Walker, that would be just a small part of their efforts to gain control. We can't let them take center stage."

Hinton, satisfied about the evidence of a Ross-Russia nexus, was finally able to ask a question.

"Why are you telling me the details of what you know? I don't work for you. I won't work for you. I have only agreed to try to find Ross."

"Right now, only Deuce and I know the details and the overall picture. We are asking you to do something that might be dangerous, and we don't want to blindside you. What we have told you may be useful in your search for Ross. Besides, we trust you to keep your mouth shut."

Now it was Deuce's turn,

"We will provide you with whatever resources you need. We know you are staying at the New Premier Inn in London, and we will be in contact shortly after you arrive. Since your flight is not for another few hours, it would be useful for you to qualify on the pistol range. When you get to London, you will be provided with a pistol and a valid UK permit."

Not for the first time, Hinton was surprised,

"This is becoming scary shit. Can I change my mind? Just kidding. I don't think I will need a pistol, but I'll be happy to qualify on the firing range. I have kept up my skills over the years. I will also need names, addresses, phone numbers, and any other contact information for the two missing analysts."

Deuce indicated that Hinton's request had been anticipated and they would give him the information. Then, he said, "Let's go to the firing range. "

The indoor range at Langley had not changed since Hinton's last visit more than twenty years earlier. It was one of several firing ranges on the Agency campus. Hinton had kept up with his skills. About once a month he went to the public firing range in Norman with one of his three pistols. His favorite was a Glock-19. With this weapon he could almost always put 8 or 9 holes in the heart or head of the paper targets at 30 yards. Not bad at all for an amateur. Now they wanted him to qualify with a much smaller weapon—one designed to be easily concealed. Hinton tested a Glock 42 and a Remington RM380. Both weapons could fit in the palm of your hand. It took Hinton a while to feel comfortable with either weapon but in less than an hour he easily passed the test and was almost up to his own standards.

Hinton told Deuce that he preferred the Glock over the RM380. His logic was simple. If he did end up shooting someone, the 9mm shells would be much more common and harder to trace than the more expensive 380s.

After finishing at the firing range, Deuce gave him a ride back to the Hyatt. Since Hinton had plenty of time on his hands before his flight to London, he found a comfortable place to sit in the lobby and called Millie, Linda, and Leslie. The conversations were not long. What could he possibly tell them? After a while, Hinton had a leisurely dinner, picked up his backpack and duffle bag from the concierge and headed across the street to the airport.

Chapter 4

London Day 1

The flight to London on Virgin Atlantic was bumpy. Hinton did not sleep much but he would not have slept very much on a smooth flight. The discussions at Langley of the three missing energy analysts and the obvious consequences of this mess had rattled him a bit. The possibility that Ross was involved and his weapon testing on the firing range were also disturbing. What bothered him most was that by the time he left, Deuce had not been able to identify the mystery woman who was apparently following him. How the hell did she decide to follow him? What was her purpose in doing so? Was Deuce not telling the truth? The most likely explanation was that she was on the Agency payroll, but that explanation did not seem to make sense. The Agency knew exactly where Hinton was and what he was doing. There was no need to follow him. Could London provide the answers?

It was just after 2 pm London time when Hinton cleared Customs and Immigration at Heathrow. Hinton then purchased a Turtle card good for a week. The Brits always had a funny way of naming things. A Turtle Card was what they called the reusable ticket for London Transport. He then boarded the tube, a misnomer since most of the ride was above-ground, and he got off at King's Cross station almost an hour later. Hinton took the slower Piccadilly Line because he wanted to check into the hotel without waiting. Hinton liked the remodeled King's Cross Station, and he was always amused by the Harry Potter exhibit and the fictional Platform 9 ¾. Kids seemed to love it and there were always children lined up to have their photo taken at the exhibit, by parents, friends, or professional photographers. Hinton had never read the Harry Potter books but he enthusiastically approved of almost anything that brought so many smiles to the faces of people of all ages.

The New Premier Inn is located on Euston Road, just three and a half blocks from King's Cross Station. Location was one of the reasons Hinton picked the hotel. Easy access to transportation is a must. In addition, the hotel is close to Russell Square, the Tavistock Hotel where Hinton knew that Ross had stayed in the past, and, not insignificantly, there are numerous restaurants and pubs nearby. This area of London was once a prime example of urban decay but was now a bustling, even prosperous area. King's Cross Station and the adjacent St. Pancras station had been remodeled more than once since the tragic fire in 1989. The station had several very good places to eat and drink. Hinton especially liked the dessert shops which sold pastries that could compete with the best. You could spend hours in the station without getting tired of it. Almost anything you might need was there.

The hotel itself lacked the charm and warmth of many fine British hotels but it was always very clean and functional. It was not designed to be charming. There was no lobby on the ground floor, only a small area and an elevator. The lobby, if you could call it that, was on the second floor which was also home to a decent restaurant. The hotel was in the middle of the block. At one end of the block was a pub and at the other end a Pret a Manger—a chain restaurant with little atmosphere but always fresh food and good coffee.

Hinton checked into the hotel and was given an envelope with a short message telling him that he would be met by someone at the pub on the corner. No time was specified. Hinton was amused that whoever had been assigned to meet him would be forced to wait in a pub for an undetermined length of time. There was also no indication of who would meet him.

Before he left the hotel, Hinton sent a text message to his friend Mohamed Aziz Rabbani, AKA the Rabbi. It was a short message. "Rabbi, where the hell are you? I am in London, and you owe me a dinner." Hinton knew that the Rabbi would respond soon. It would be good to get together again with his old friend.

Hinton had known the Rabbi since their graduate school days at the University of Texas. Hinton was already in his second year of the PhD program when the Rabbi showed up in Austin. Hinton assumed that Mohamed was just another rich Saudi who was in Austin to play. He was wrong. The Rabbi was a serious scholar and a hell-of-a-good guy. Yes, the Rabbi had a lot more money than other graduate students but he never flaunted it. The Rabbi was quickly accepted as just another member of the gang. How could any of us reject him when he was almost instantly given the nickname Rabbi and seemed to enjoy it? These days, the Rabbi was the Deputy Minister of Energy in the Kingdom, just one step down from Abdul Aziz Salmon, the energy minister. The Rabbi was so talented that he survived when his former boss, Ali al-Naemi had been fired as Energy Minister in 2016. The Rabbi split most of his time between London and Riyadh. The Rabbi also knew Ross. If Ross were in London, the chances were high that the Rabbi would know where he was and what he was doing.

When Hinton left the hotel, he turned left on Euston Street rather than turning right to go directly to the pub. He stopped briefly at the graveyard that was part of St. Pancras New Church and then continued his walk along Euston. The New Church was approaching its 200th birthday and was a bit run-down but it was much newer than the nearby

Old Church. Three blocks down the street he crossed to the opposite side and stood near a bus-stop for several minutes. Satisfied that he was not being followed, Hinton reversed himself and walked to the pub.

As Hinton crossed Euston Road, he saw Chuck Johnston sitting at one of the small outside tables at the pub. Of course, the Agency would send someone recognizable to meet him. Hinton sat down at the table and asked Johnston how long he had been there. Johnston's reply was that he had been there about a pint and a half, not exactly a length of time but it did convey the right information. Johnston said that there had been no additional sightings of Ross, so Hinton's assignment remained the same. There had also been no new developments in Patti Walker's murder case. The DC police and the FBI were stymied. Ross remained the only person of interest. Johnston also confirmed that the mystery woman who had apparently followed Hinton in DC was not from the Agency. They had no idea who she was despite video coverage of her at the airport Hyatt. Facial recognition software, usually reliable, had not helped.

When the waiter finally arrived, Hinton ordered a pint as well as fish and chips. He had not eaten in a long time. Johnston also ordered another pint and, like Hinton, the fish and chips. It turned out that the two had something in common. They were both Cub fans. Hinton was surprised about how well-informed Johnston was about the Cubs. There was nothing fake about his knowledge. This was not something the Agency had cooked up to bind the two together. Johnston was impressed with how Hinton's dog Fergie got his name. He already knew who was taking care of the dog in Oklahoma. Johnston knew too damned much about him. Johnston knew a lot about Hinton's ex-wife Linda, about Millie, Billie Joe and even their two daughters. He knew that all of them loved West Texas, Big Bend National Park, and country music.

Johnston revealed little about himself. He had been with the Agency about a decade. He was a Stanford graduate in computer science, but he did not specify whether his Stanford education was undergraduate or graduate studies. Beyond his confession of being a Cubs fan, Johnston revealed almost nothing about his personal life. Despite the small talk, Johnston was still the cautious, thoroughly professional Agency type.

Johnston told Hinton that when they were finished that he should take the small soft-leather briefcase sitting below the table. Inside the case were several useful items including detailed information about the two missing London energy analysts, a rather large sum of cash, a Glock 43 with several clips of ammunition, a concealed carry permit valid in the UK and throughout the EU, and identification as a US Air Marshall. The cash consisted of both large and small bills in pounds, Euros, and US dollars. There was also a burner phone, but Johnston did not think Hinton would need it since he would need to use his own phone if he tried to call or text Ross. Four numbers had been programmed into the burner phone, one each for Johnston, the two missing analysts, and an emergency number if Johnston for some reason did not answer. Hinton was told to add these numbers to the contact list on his own phone. Johnston and Ross agreed to meet at the pub every day, but no specific time was specified.

Hinton thought all of this was overkill. After all, he was only looking for a colleague who had apparently disappeared. After finishing the fish and chips, which were not bad for pub food, Hinton returned to his room at the hotel. He put some of the cash in his wallet, programmed the four numbers on the burner phone into his own, put the Glock and an extra clip into the pocket of the specially designed blazer he had been given at Langley, and decided it was too early to hit the sack despite his fatigue.

Hinton walked to the Tavistock Hotel. It was a pleasant walk in the early evening. In a way, it was a homecoming. Hinton had stayed there many times and he knew that Ross stayed there frequently as well. Hinton liked the place but had switched to the newer Premier Inn because the Tavistock needed more than just a little renovation. In fact, the Tavistock's main attractions were its low price and convenient location. Reviews of the aging facility inevitably described it as lacking modern amenities and lacking the cleanliness that most travelers take for granted.

The desk clerk at the Tavistock, a young man of Pakistani descent named Sadiq, recognized Hinton immediately and with a smile on his face said, "Professor Hinton, it is good to see you. I hope you are doing well. Unfortunately, the hotel is full for the next two nights."

Hinton remembered that it had been Sadiq who had first recommended the Premier Inn to him when on an earlier trip the hotel was also full. Hinton explained that he did not need a room that night. He was only looking for his friend Ross. Sadiq's response was unsettling.

"Ross must be a popular man. Ross was here late last week but only for one night. He checked in under the name John Douglas dropping Ross altogether. Later Ross gave me 50 quid not to correct this omission. Since then, you are the third person to inquire about him. I don't know where he has gone. Maybe he found a new girlfriend. Maybe he joined the BDSM Society and is participating in their annual convention."

Hinton was unfamiliar with the BDSM Society. Sadiq explained, "BDSM means Bondage, Discipline, and Sado Masochism. The BDSM Society is holding their annual convention and that is why the hotel is full. The Society owns an office building on the other side of Russell Square. The Society occupies the basement and first floor. The rest of the building is rented out. The sign in the small lobby of the first floor simply says private offices. The Society operates all year long, but the annual convention attracts many of the Society's members who live outside of London. At the end of the convention, special prizes will be awarded in several categories. What do they do at the convention? They do what you might expect. They play B&D and S&M games and enjoy themselves with other diversions. The Society has strict rules so that no one will be injured. The Society is well-known to the London Police and Scotland Yard, but nothing they do is illegal under British law or London ordinances. Several high-ranking members of both organizations are members of the Society. Society members never seem to cause anyone trouble. Hotel management welcomes them because they often pay for rooms that are unoccupied for days at a time."

Hinton was more than a little perplexed and asked, "Why do you think Ross might be participating in the Society's annual convention?" Sadiq told Hinton that Ross had been in long conversations in the lobby with the president of the group who kept a room at the hotel on a permanent basis. When Sadiq offered Hinton a card that would at least get him in the door, Hinton put the card in his coat-pocket, but he had no intention of using it.

"Sadiq, you seem to know a lot about this Society. Are you a member?"

"Absolutely not. I might be curious about it, but Society membership is expensive: 2,500 pounds for a year or 300 pounds per month."

Hinton was more interested in the two people who had inquired about Ross. Sadiq told him that he did not know their names, but one was a man in his late thirties or early forties and the other was a woman about the same age. Sadiq was expecting a large tip from Hinton, which he got soon enough, so he offered to bring up the two Ross chasers on CCTV.

While the hotel itself had not been updated recently, cameras and hard disk drives were cheap. The hotel had installed cameras in the lobby, the front desk, and the front door. Sadiq took great pride in the modern technology, which had become common throughout London and elsewhere in the UK. CCTV solved a lot of problems for the management of hotels, restaurants, bars, and shops that dealt with the public.

With a few clicks of the computer mouse, Sadiq brought up video of the man who had asked about Ross. Hinton had no trouble identifying the man. Chuck Johnston was not disguised in any way. A few more clicks of the mouse and video of the woman appeared. Hinton was not positive about her identity, but she could have been the mystery woman who seemed to have followed him in DC. Without too much trouble, Sadiq took screen shots of the woman from three different angles and sent the images to Hinton's phone.

Hinton gave Sadiq a generous tip of 100 pounds. Sadiq had been very cooperative, and Hinton thought he deserved a large tip, especially since the money was Agency money. It was worth it and Sadiq seemed pleased. Hinton was confident that both Johnston and the woman had also given Sadiq large tips. It was likely that Sadiq was making more money from these off-the-record activities than from his regular employment. Good for him.

Hinton had a huge smile on his face as he left Sadiq and headed for the door of the Tavistock. By the time he was outside, his smile had turned into a full-blown laugh. He realized that he had not smiled or laughed enough since this peculiar adventure started last Friday. He liked to laugh but generally not at the expense of someone else. In this case, it was just the thought of Ross having anything to do with the BDSM Society. It was so implausible that Hinton could not do anything but

40

laugh. Still, he crossed Tavistock Square and headed for the address Sadiq had given him, an office building near Russell Square.

The building was a boring looking three-story structure probably constructed in the 1960s. Hinton snapped a photo of the place on his cell phone and then walked slowly past the building. The building was indistinguishable from others in the area. The glass doors at the entrance to the lobby revealed a security guard sitting behind a mahogany or fake mahogany desk. There was only one small sign on the building indicating that the top floor was occupied by a firm called London Energy Consultants. Hinton had never heard of this firm but there were probably hundreds of firms devoted to giving advice and myths to oil and gas companies and governments. He would need to find out more about exactly who they were and what they did. Hinton was tired but he took the time to walk around the block and take a second look at the headquarters of the BDSM Society. He did not expect to see Ross or anyone else he knew exit the building. His expectations were fulfilled. Just in case, he called Chuck Johnston and informed him of his conversation with Sadiq. Within an hour a small, hardly noticeable video camera had been placed on a sign across the street from the BDSM Society building. The video signal was broadcast to a car parked nearby. Every thirty minutes, the non-descript driver of the car stopped by and loaded the video on a flash drive which was then examined by Embassy personnel for any sign of Ross.

Hinton had a lot to think about on the way back to the New Premier Inn. He understood completely that he was not a detective. He had been recruited by the Agency only to find his colleague Ross, not to solve a murder mystery or anything larger. Still, finding Ross might lead him into dangerous territory. The corporations and governments with trillions of dollars tied up in oil played hardball, not some kid's game. Would

41

they kill or hire a professional to kill someone who threatened their interests? Yes, of course. They had done so many times in the past and if you were a serious threat they would come after your family and friends as well. Hinton understood that he was playing a dangerous game and that he should be careful.

Hinton would continue his attempts to find Ross, but he would trust no one. He was still convinced that Ross was an unlikely suspect in the murder of Patti Walker and the disappearance of the other two energy analysts. Patti Walker's murder could have been a random crime which the DC police might eventually solve. Or not. The payments to Ross could be merely to ensure that his forthcoming book painted the Russian industry in a favorable light.

Hinton had no clue who the mystery woman was, and he had less than full confidence that he could trust Chuck Johnston or anyone else from the Agency. The safest thing to do was to assume that everyone he had contact with was an actual or potential threat. He would need a way out – some means of separating himself from this whole messy business.

The flight from DC and the events of the last few days were catching up with him. Sleep was in order, and he was glad to see the New Premier Inn on Euston Road. When he got to his room, he checked his duffle bag to make certain that no one had opened it. The bag had not been tampered with. Although it was only 8:30 pm London time, Hinton promptly fell asleep knowing that he would be able to cope with a complicated situation better in the morning.

Chapter 5
London Days 2 and 3

Hinton woke up early. He arrived at Pret a Manger at 6 am just as they were opening. He ordered a breakfast sandwich, a banana, and a cup of French roast coffee that was far better than the coffee he had made in the hotel. After the quick breakfast, he walked the short distance to King's Cross Station, boarded a train on the Circle Line, changed at Victoria Station and exited at the Sloane Square Station. He was now only a few short blocks from 98 Eaton Place, where Cindy Burgess, one of the two missing analysts, lived. Hinton just wanted to know what it looked like and to see if there was any activity in the building. He did not anticipate finding Cindy or anyone else during his visit.

Eaton Place was only a few blocks long. The buildings were two story residences, almost all of them painted white. This was expensive real estate where diplomats and upper management in corporations lived. Like the other buildings in the area, number 98 was well kept and well maintained. A short flight of concrete steps led to the front door. Hinton walked well past number 98, turned around and pretended to answer his cell phone. He stood there three or four minutes just watching, knowing that he would not look suspicious while holding a cell phone to his ear. He then walked past number 98 on the other side of the street and again reached for his cell phone.

Much to Hinton's surprise, he saw a woman opening the front door to Cindy's house. She began sweeping the steps. Hinton approached her and told the woman he was looking for Cindy. The woman looked at Hinton with suspicion until he handed her a business card and told her that he was a professional colleague. The woman then told Hinton that she had not seen Cindy in several days. This was not unusual, she explained. Cindy often traveled on business and although she usually left her a note explaining where she had gone, this time she had not done so. The cleaner became talkative and said that she worked for several people on the street, but that Cindy was the kindest of the bunch. After a minute or two of small talk, Hinton retrieved his business card and wrote "Please call me" on the limited white space. It was a long shot, but Hinton thought Cindy might call if she returned. The cleaner promised to place the card on the kitchen counter by the phone.

Hinton thanked the woman and walked slowly to Sloane Square. He was reasonably certain that he was not being followed. That did not stop him from taking the usual precautions to make certain. About a block from the station, he stopped at a small grocery shop, lingered a few minutes, and then bought a small package of cookies before returning to the street. The station was to the left as he exited the grocery store, but he looked to the right before proceeding. Hinton recognized no one in that direction but just as he was approaching the station, he saw someone who was either the mystery woman or her twin sister. Hinton tried to catch up with her, but she had already entered the station. By the time he got to the platform, she was already gone.

Who the hell was she? Hinton had no idea, but he promised himself that he would find out. He took the next train to Victoria Station but did not transfer to the Victoria line as he had intended. Instead, He left the metro and started to walk. Hinton did not linger at Victoria Station even though he had been tempted to do so. Several years ago, he had run into a friend at Victoria Station, a random encounter that later he learned was a surprisingly common event. If you wanted to find someone in London, especially an American, there were two obvious places to look: Victoria Station and the international terminal at Heathrow. Although he was not in a hurry, he did not want to spend time hanging around either place. He wanted to see where Diane Stoddard, the other missing energy analyst, lived.

Hinton walked from Victoria Station to St. James Park and then past Westminster Abbey. He would cross the river on Westminster Bridge. This journey was not far, even with the detour through St. James Park, it was only a little over a mile. At mid-morning there would be a lot of people milling about or deliberately going somewhere. The important thing was that this walk was unplanned and unpredictable. No one could anticipate where he was heading, and it would give Hinton the opportunity to take in one of his favorite London views: the Houses of Parliament from the middle of Westminster Bridge. The architecture, the history, the river, and maybe the fact that it was a familiar place attracted Hinton to the bridge.

At the middle of the bridge, Hinton turned around to take in the view. Instead, what caught his attention was a small white van speeding up the bridge as if it were aimed right at him. Instinctively, Hinton moved quickly to avoid the van, which jumped the curb and ran into several people on the bridge. Hinton reached for the Glock but did not remove it from his pocket. The scene was chaos. There were simply too many people nearby for the Glock to do any good. Some of the pedestrians had already surrounded the driver of the van. Within seconds, police were rushing up the bridge and Hinton wisely decided to get out of the area. Later, he would learn that five people had been killed by the van and eleven more injured. The London authorities caught the driver and would later report that he was a Syrian and a member of ISIS.

At the end of the bridge, Hinton crossed the street and found a very empty Starbucks next to the Metro stop. He bought a cup of Pike Place, his favorite, and crossed the street again. He soon found a bench near Westminster Abbey and sat down. Hinton had never been able to walk and drink coffee at the same time. He had already concluded that the incident on the bridge had nothing to do with him. Still, the van had seemed to be aimed directly at him. Probably not. No one would know where he was, at least not in time to plan something like that. The coffee would help him think. He smiled when he thought that other people might think it odd to sit and drink coffee after confronting danger.

He did not care much about what other people thought and he knew that most of them had not grown up in West Texas where danger was simply a part of everyday life. Hinton was not generally frightened of physical danger, but he had a healthy respect for it. He had faced physical danger many times. As a teenager, he had participated in always dangerous rodeo events and even a couple of knife fights. Rattlesnakes, javelinas, scorpions, and other critters in West Texas did not bother him. Once he had been within a couple of hundred yards of a tornado. He did not seek out danger but what can best be described as West Texas fatalism, an acceptance of danger as part of life, had served him well.

As he sat there, pondering his next steps, the mystery woman walked in front of him. No, he was not imagining things. There she was, not 30 feet away. He mumbled a quick "God Damn" and got up to follow her. Hinton had no chance of following her. She was gone, nowhere to be found. His failure amused him, intensified his curiosity, and made him very mad.

While he preferred public transport, Hinton took a taxi, a classic old-style black London taxi not a ride-share. The famous old-style taxis had been devastated by the rise of the ride-share industry. Hinton wondered how long the black taxis could survive. He gave the driver instructions to drop him at the British Museum. Taxis could be traced and there was no point in giving his actual destination. From the British Museum it was only a short walk to Regents Canal which was one of his favorite places in London. A visit to Diane Stoddard's flat could wait. The canal stretched for eight or nine miles with a footpath, once a towpath for the barges, along most of it. In concentrated areas, there were several bars, restaurants, and shops. Hinton was always pleased by the book boat, the only floating bookstore in London. He would use the peaceful surroundings to make some overdue phone calls.

His first call was to the Rabbi to confirm dinner plans for 7:30 that evening. It was a short conversation. There was no need to discuss where to eat. For years, they had met at the same Indian restaurant, Woburn Tandoori on, where else, Woburn Walk. There were better Indian food restaurants in London, but they had been meeting there for so long that any other place was not on the list. Woburn Walk was a delight. The short street was narrow and was often described as something Dickens could have written about. The restaurant itself was small with even smaller white-linen covered tables. The fact that this Indian restaurant was run by Bangladeshis, not Indians, added to the charm. The naan was as good as could be found anywhere. The Tandoori chicken not so much. Hinton preferred the chicken curry.

After the call to the Rabbi, Hinton called, emailed, and sent a text to Ross. He did not expect a reply. That would have been far too simple.

After a short walk along the canal Hinton came to another quiet place and called Millie who answered on the second ring and cheerfully said, "How are you, cowboy?"

Happy to hear her voice, Hinton replied, "I am happier than a tornado in a trailer park. It is a beautiful day in London, but I am making

47

no progress on finding Ross. What about you?"

"No, I have had no luck either. I call, text, and email him every day but get no response. Yesterday I left a message telling him that he would be fired if he did not respond. Still no response. Ross probably knows that I can't fire him, but I thought it might let him know that my requests were serious."

Millie seemed almost too happy to hear from him. They talked for a few minutes about the girls, Fergie, and some trivial goings on at the university. Hinton knew that he could not hide much of anything from Millie and after a while he described his encounter with the van.

Millie was not amused and replied, sternly, "I will be really pissed if you manage to get yourself killed over this silly business. The possibility of inheriting Fergie, a jeep, and a paid-for house, much less a second daughter does not appeal to me at all. You are to return safely and quickly."

"You are in my will Millie, but don't get too excited. I am a lot harder to kill than you might think."

The conversation ended and Hinton spent the next hour or so walking along the canal doing his best not to think about Millie, Ross, or what he was doing in this messy situation. "Can I change my mind?" was a thought that occurred to him more than once. Eventually, he returned to the hotel, charged his cell phone battery, and left to meet Johnston at the pub. He went straight to the pub without taking any precautions about being followed. His precautions were ineffective. The mystery woman found him and maybe the driver of the van on the bridge found him. He was convinced that someone was following him on the canal. Why bother to take precautions?

Johnston was late arriving at the pub. When he did arrive thirty minutes late, both men ordered a pint. Hinton waited deliberately for

Johnston to begin the conversation. After an awkward silence Johnston began,

"Ross was captured on camera exiting the BDSM Society building with Diane Stoddard. Both looked happy or at least amused. The Agency was able to access CCTV videos for two or three blocks, but they suddenly vanished from the cameras. We have no idea where they are now. I also have no news about Cindy Burgess. By the way, I know about the incident with the van this morning, but I don't think it had anything to do with you."

When Hinton finally spoke, he calmly said, "Call off the mystery woman. If you don't, I am done, and you can look for Ross on your own."

"I can assure you that the mystery woman is not Agency. We are as befuddled as you are about who she is or why she might be following you. We will continue to use our resources to find out who she is."

"I hope you are telling me the truth. I can become a really mean son-of-a-bitch if I think you are lying to me. What about the Patti Walker case?"

"There is no progress on finding Patti Walker's killer. Ross is still the most likely suspect."

The conversation had been tense. Hinton ended it by noting that the Cubs three game sweep of Milwaukee placed them in a tie for first place with the evil Cardinals. They agreed to meet at the same time and place tomorrow.

At 7:30 Hinton arrived at the Woburn Tandoori restaurant. Much to his surprise, the Rabbi who was almost always late was already seated. As always, Hinton and the Rabbi exchanged family news. Shabazz and the kids were fine. Shabazz was in Paris spending more money than she should but would meet the Rabbi in Vienna next week for the OPEC+

meetings. Another tradition was followed as well. The Rabbi had to remind Hinton unnecessarily, of course, that they had both pursued Shabazz while they were in graduate school. Shabazz, a graduate student in political science from Morocco, was the most gorgeous woman either of them had ever seen. She was also smarter than either one of them. In the end, the Rabbi was the winner. Diplomatically, the Rabbi did not ask Hinton about his failed marriage.

The Rabbi had not seen or heard from Ross. "But I have an idea," he exclaimed, "Why don't you come to Vienna next week. You know that Ross rarely misses an OPEC meeting. We could have a great time and you could find out first-hand about any major policy changes in the energy world. I will see to it that you have credentials and access to the people who can tell you what you want to know. Shabazz would love to see you. Just let me know where you are going to be staying and I will have credentials delivered to you. If Ross is around, I am sure that you will find him."

Hinton readily agreed. Even if Ross turned up before the meetings, it would be great fun to see Shabazz and to learn what he could at the OPEC meetings.

During the meal, Hinton mentioned the extra security that the Rabbi seemed to have brought with him. Most people would have thought that the man and woman seated at a table near the window of the restaurant were just another couple out for dinner, if they had been noticed at all. Anyone with some training would have identified them quickly as security. Hinton had noticed the thinly disguised pistol in the man's coat, which was not as well tailored as his own. The Rabbi was not pleased that Hinton had spotted them so easily but then admitted that several high-level members of the Saudi energy community had received threats in recent weeks. Saudi intelligence considered the threats to be genuine and had mandated the extra security. Shabazz too had been assigned a security detail on her shopping trip to Paris.

Hinton asked the Rabbi if the threats were related to the rumors about a major change in Saudi energy policy and economic development strategy. The Rabbi admitted that this was possible, but he could not discuss the details of the new Saudi strategy yet – even with an old friend. After the announcements in Vienna, he could talk. He added that he was saddened by the death of Patti Walker. She had been helping the Kingdom with the new strategy. And, he added: "No, we did not kill her."

The two old friends ended the meal on a higher note. Hinton agreed again that he would go to Vienna in the next day or two and would make certain that the Rabbi knew where to find him. Hinton looked forward to seeing Shabazz and to learning what the Saudi's were up to.

The next morning, Hinton was late getting up. Maybe the pressure of travel and the events of the last few days had caught up with him. By ten o'clock, he had barely finished breakfast at Pret a Manger when his cell phone rang. It was Johnston, who said they had to meet at once. They agreed to meet in thirty minutes at a coffee shop in King's Cross station.

Hinton arrived first. When Johnston sat down a couple of minutes later, he appeared agitated and wasted no time in starting the conversation.

"It is even more urgent that we find Ross. We need to find him now. Diane Stoddard is dead. She was found about two hours ago by the proprietor of an off-the-books bed and breakfast near Heathrow. Like Patti Walker, it was a brutal killing, possibly staged to look like a sexual assault gone wrong. Only Patti's killer or someone associated with the investigation could have done this. There is no point in describing some

51

of the most gruesome details, but one example is that both Diane and Patti were found nude and tied up spread-eagled on a bed. An odd thing is that the left hands of both women were tied not to the corner of the bed but to their left thighs. The knots were simple hitch knots but very similar and very well done. It had to be the same killer or killers in both cases. We are searching world-wide for similar cases at any time in the last five years. There is nothing yet."

Johnston continued without giving Hinton a chance to speak. "There has been no progress on the Patti Walker case. There has been no sign of Cindy Burgess. There have been no additional sightings of Ross. We keep hearing rumors about major Saudi policy moves and we know that both women were working with the Saudis. No one has been able to identify the mystery woman. We are completely stymied."

When he was finally given the opportunity to speak, Hinton described his meeting with the Rabbi and told Johnston he was going to go to Vienna. Johnston quickly agreed and said he would make the travel arrangements. In the meantime, Hinton should continue to look for Ross in London.

Chapter 6

Paris

Early on Friday morning, Hinton packed his duffle bag for the trip to Vienna. The night before, he had returned the Glock and the burner phone to Johnston and explained that Millie had made his travel arrangements. He knew that a weapon in Vienna would be more of a nuisance than an asset. Security at OPEC headquarters was strict, and he would be unable to enter the building with a weapon even with credentials supplied by the Rabbi. While he had not used the weapon in London, carrying it had given him a comfortable almost peaceful feeling. Without it he felt like something was missing. This strange feeling was not that he felt naked without it. Rather, it was more like he had worn socks of different colors or forgotten to zip his fly, which he checked before leaving the room and heading for Pret a Manger for breakfast.

Hinton looked forward to Pret for more than the food. The young woman behind the counter was delightful. Hinton had learned during their first encounter several days earlier that Rose was a student at the London School of Economics. In her mid-twenties, she had been born in Nigeria and had been in London for less than two years. In turn, Rose learned that Hinton was an economics professor from the U.S. She had a smile that always made Hinton feel better. A couple of days later, during her thirty-minute break, she asked Hinton for some help with an econometrics problem. In just a few minutes, Hinton had explained the concept of simultaneous equations bias. Rose was more than happy with finally understanding something that had bothered her for most of the semester.

Rather than simply disappearing, he told Rose of his plans, "I am going to Paris for a couple of days and then to Vienna. I plan to return in a few days. When I get back, I want to talk to you about the OU PhD program in economics. When you complete your master's degree at London School of Economics, the OU program would be a great opportunity and you would be an asset to the program. I would like to recruit you to come join us."

"I am honored, Professor I have only been in the US once, last week to attend a conference. LSE paid for the trip as they do once a year for all graduate students. LSE wants their graduate students to be exposed to the wider academic world. I was only in DC three days and was supposed to attend as many conference sessions as possible. On the second day of the conference, I could not resist taking a tour of DC on the double-decker tour buses that allowed you to get on or off at any stop. I loved the tour but was deeply saddened by the number of monuments and memorials to various wars. I am excited by the possibility of seeing more of the US and studying at a new university."

Rose did not quite understand Hinton's puzzled look. Hinton had realized that Rose was in DC at the time of Patti Walker's murder and was back in London in plenty of time to be involved in the disappearance of the two other energy analysts. He wondered if this was even possible. Rose was a very bright young woman who was intent on finishing her degree at LSE. How could she be involved? Hinton dismissed the idea, but Rose's story reminded him that there could be any number of plausible suspects in Patti Walker's murder and that he must keep an open mind. When Rose asked him about the odd look on his face, Hinton said that he too was often disturbed by the war memorials in DC, especially the Viet Nam memorial.

A few minutes later, Hinton left Pret and returned to his hotel to retrieve his bags. The night before he had called Millie to confirm his reservations on the train, two nights in Paris, and three nights in Vienna. After Vienna, his plan was to return to London and then back to the States—whether he had found Ross or not. He was getting tired of this whole business. Yes, he enjoyed being in London and he was confident that a day or two in Paris would be refreshing but the search for Ross should be conducted by professionals. His intellectual curiosity about the mystery woman, the murders, and the change in Saudi energy policy intrigued him but he was a long way from convincing himself that he could be successful. The cost of being involved was high. For the first time he knew that he really belonged in Oklahoma or Texas. He missed the comforting routine of a walk with Fergie each morning, his students, Millie, and Linda, and writing something each day. Despite how long he had known Ross, they were not close friends. Why should he really care about something which could only lead to trouble? Again, he asked himself if he could change his mind.

For now, he could walk the short distance to St. Pancras Station and not worry about his reason for being in Europe for a few days. Hinton liked trains and rarely turned down the chance to go by train if that was an option. He had traveled by train on several continents including what he thought were exotic trips. He had taken the highest altitude standard gauge train in the world from Lima to Huancayo. One of his favorites was the narrow-gauge railway to Darjeeling. But Hinton had never been on the Eurostar through the Chunnel. He would soon remedy that void in his experience, and he was looking forward to it. His train did not leave until 2 pm. In the meantime, he could find a comfortable place to sit at St. Pancras and begin to write what he thought would be a hell of a good article about energy policy, including the dark side of the oil industry.

The Eurostar was sleek, modern, and very fast. He knew from the brochure he had picked up that the Eurostar would deliver him to Paris, a distance of about 250 miles, in just under two and a half hours. The rest of his journey to Vienna would be much longer and much slower. At his request, he had been assigned a window seat. The trip through the Chunnel was only about 25 miles and took little time at 100 miles per hour, the slowest portion of the trip. Once in France the train was a lot faster. Hinton looked out the window but found the views less than satisfying at 185 miles per hour. This was better than a plane, the cheapest and fastest way to travel from London to Vienna, but not by much.

Hinton left the Gare du Nord wondering what made Paris so different from London. Paris just feels different, he thought. It was not the language. It was not the culture, whatever that meant. It was not even the food—not any longer. Britain was part of the EU, at least for now, and London too had great cuisine. This was not a puzzle that could be solved in the short walk from the train station to Hotel Terminus Nord, which was the first thing anyone saw upon leaving the station. The hotel had little to recommend it to the average tourist, but it was near Gare du Nord, moderately priced by Paris standards, and clean. Millie had done well in selecting it for him.

Hinton checked in, noticed both the bar and restaurant in the lobby and took the elevator to his third-floor room. As he opened the door, he could sense but not see someone else in the room. Instead of following his instinct to turn around and run, he entered the room. Without thinking, he reached for the Glock but before his hand reached his coat pocket, he realized that it was no longer there. He half expected the mystery woman, or some hired assassin to be in the room, but Millie stepped out from behind the door and gave him a warm hug and a kiss on the cheek.

"Goddamn Millie you scared the shit out of me." Were the first words Hinton could manage and then he said: "What the hell are you doing here?"

Millie's response was calm and most likely rehearsed. With a sly smile she replied, "I thought you might be happy to see me after being gone so long."

Hinton was happy to see her but with as much contrived anger as he could muster, he said, "You didn't answer my question. What the hell are you doing here?"

Millie was not fooled easily. She knew that Hinton was not really angry. Despite their long friendship, she had only seen him genuinely pissed a couple of times and on both occasions Hinton simply went silent. Still smiling, Millie said she had reason enough to be in his room in a Paris hotel and that she might be willing to share those reasons over an early dinner. She was famished.

The two friends left the hotel and walked several blocks stopping to read the menu at each café and restaurant they passed. They did not find a place to eat that appealed to them. The restaurant with the most interesting menu was not even open for dinner yet. It was just before 5 pm Paris time—far too early for most locals to eat an evening meal. Hinton's suggestion that they keep walking was met with a disapproving look from Millie. She suggested returning to the hotel, where the sign at the entrance to the restaurant indicated that it was open 24 hours a day. Reluctantly, Hinton agreed.

There were no other customers in the restaurant, so the waiter did not object to Hinton's request to be seated at a table next to a window. Once seated, Hinton spoke in French, confident that Millie would not understand most of the conversation. He explained to the waiter that he had promised his beautiful companion a truly excellent meal and even better wine. If you disappoint us, I am certain that she will not sleep with me for at least a week. Without saying so, Hinton knew that Millie would not sleep with him no matter how good the meal and wine happened to be. The waiter acknowledged his understanding and approval with a smile. He turned and walked away without saying a word, returning very quickly with a bottle of Rhone and some bread as a starter.

Millie and Hinton approved of the smooth, light, red wine which would go well with almost any meal. The waiter left menus, recommended the fixed price dinner, and left them in peace to decide on a meal. Hinton wanted to take the opportunity to press Millie on why she had come to Paris on short notice, but he knew Millie better than that. She would tell him when she was ready and no sooner.

After the bread and some wine, they ordered from the prix fixe menu consisting of a salad, a soup, a main course, a choice of desserts and coffee. Hinton tried to think of a bad meal he had had anywhere in France, but nothing came to mind. Hinton's main course was steak with pepper sauce. Millie's choice was *coq au vin*. She told Hinton that she had prepared this meal a couple of dozen times but looked forward to having it for the first time in France. They would not be disappointed by the meal.

Eventually, the waiter brought the salad and Millie talked about the reasons for her trip. "I am not here to have sex with you, no matter how tempting that might be. As you may have noticed, I have the adjoining room so you can forget whatever ideas you might have on your mind. I am not ready to spoil our relationship. We want you to come home. This is far too dangerous, and Ross is just not worth the risk."

Hinton asked who was included in "we" and Millie continued, "My trip started after a series of events on campus. On Monday, Gary Ford had his regular weekly meeting with President Henderson. He mentioned that he needed you to convene the athletic appeals committee and for the first time ever, you were nowhere to be found. A star volleyball player tested positive for the nasty weed, and she is appealing her suspension from the team. Dean Crowley then met with the president and told him he needed you to meet with a representative from the oil and gas association. They are willing to establish endowed chairs for you, Ross, and a faculty member of our choice. No strings attached and the endowments would be worth millions. They wanted to meet with you and Henderson before announcing anything. The list goes on. Two of your graduate students have filed sexual harassment charges against Professor Milton. They are willing to talk to you before leaking this to the press."

Hinton interjected, "Millie this is all bullshit. We both know that nothing happens rapidly at the university—this one or any other university. Very little is urgent at OU. The university moves on a geologic time scale. I will concede that the fire department responding to a fire in one of the high-rise dorms housing a thousand students might be considered urgent but damned little else. So, tell me what this is about."

Millie started talking again. "The president called me into his office after the other meetings. He had heard about Diane Stoddard's murder from a tiny article in the Washington Post. The same source told him about the van attack on Westminster Bridge. He asked me if you were the target. I admitted that you were very close but that there was no reason to believe that you had been targeted. He asked me what else I knew, and I told him about the mystery woman and that you were

59

carrying a pistol. I know I should not have told him anything, but I couldn't lie to him. Needless to say, the president was not pleased."

Hinton noticed a young woman that the waiter had seated a few tables away. Hinton looked at her twice and Millie responded with a frown and a teasing reprimand suggesting that it was impolite to have dinner with one woman and to stare at another. They both laughed a little and Millie continued her story.

"Henderson trusts me enough to think out loud. He knows I would not reveal anything without his permission. He confessed that he had made a mistake by encouraging you to get involved in trying to find Ross. He thought Ross was probably a lost cause, but he did not want to lose two faculty members, especially when one of them is you. He wanted to get you back on campus, but he knew that if he demanded your return that you would react by becoming even more determined to play detective. Then, he asked if I would be willing to use our long-standing friendship to change your mind."

"I told him that I too wanted you to return but was not quite certain how I could accomplish that. The president then surprised me more than a little. He told me that I should go to London and confront you directly. He thought that you would have a more difficult time saying no if I were standing in front of you. I told him that you would be in Paris by the time I could get there. He then told me he didn't care if you were in Rio or Mogadishu, it was time for you to return."

Millie was an expert at travel arrangements. The president informed her that she could not travel on the university's dime but that if she were willing to go, he would reimburse her from his own pocket. Millie told him that she had plenty of frequent flyer miles and would use them for the airfare. He insisted on paying for any other expenses and Millie did not object. Millie's story was not complete, and she continued.

"I really want you to come home. I have no desire to take care of two houses, two daughters and a dog if you get yourself killed. Fergie sits by the front door for most of every day. I am sure she is waiting for you to open the door and take her for a walk. I want you back, the president wants you back, if Linda and the girls knew what you were doing, they would insist that you come home. In any case, I am here and almost begging you to return. By the way, quit glancing at that young woman."

Hinton did not respond. Instead, he signaled for the waiter who was standing several feet away. When the waiter came to the table Hinton handed him his cell phone and asked the waiter to take several pictures of them at the table. Hinton knew that the young woman would be perfectly framed by the two of them. When the waiter returned his phone, Hinton looked at the digital images. Two of them included perfect views of the young woman. He thanked the waiter, smiled, and sent them to Chuck Johnston who would know what to do with them without being told.

Later, they headed back to the room. On the way, Hinton remembered a night at the Chisos Basin Lodge in Big Bend when he and Millie had spent the night in the same bed without anything more sexual than a quick kiss on the cheek. Billie was still alive then and to say that the four of them trusted each other was an understatement. In Big Bend, Billie had been called back to the office and through a colossal series of mistakes they had ended up with only one room. This time, Billie was gone and there was no reason to avoid the obvious fact that they had always been attracted to each other. Hinton wondered what Millie was thinking but he knew instinctively not to ask. He would find out soon enough. Maybe they would just drink the second bottle of Rhone that Millie had ordered to take out.

When they entered the room, Hinton checked the small closet, the bathroom, and the adjoining room just to make certain that they were alone. He also checked his bag to make certain that it had not been tampered with. It was an easy thing to arrange an open bottle of shampoo or mouthwash inside a bag in such a way that any movement of the bag or attempt to open it would cause the bottle to spill. There were other ways of setting this up and Hinton had used most of them over the years, but the bottle trap was almost impossible to foil. He also did a systematic search of the room looking for cameras or microphones. He found nothing but knew that the technology was so advanced that he might have missed something. Everything was in good order, so Hinton retrieved a couple of glasses for the wine.

Hinton was in a good mood. He now thought that he had been wrong earlier in concluding that Millie would not have sex with him. He now anticipated a long-awaited evening of great sex with someone he cared deeply about. He dismissed the inevitable complications this would cause. They were both adults. There would be no need to apologize or explain their new relationship – not even to their daughters. Just go with the flow.

Millie quickly and firmly let him know that this would not be a night of great sex or any other kind of sex. She knew exactly what was on Hinton's mind and agenda but wanted no part of it. She reminded him of the unwritten and unspoken rules of their relationship. They could talk and even tease each other about anything but a sexual relationship would destroy what they had. She was not ready for that. Once again, as in Big Bend, they would sleep together but there would be no sex. They finished the bottle of Rhone. They did not order another.

Hinton understood what Millie had said but he was perplexed. He knew her well enough to also understand that soon, if not now, their

62

relationship had to change. It might turn into a sexual relationship with long-lasting implications. It might not. Perhaps their relationship would end altogether. The status quo was not a realistic possibility. Hinton was not a mind-reader, but he was very confident that Millie understood this as well as he did. For tonight, sleep was in order and tomorrow he would do his best to show Millie around Paris.

By the time they fell asleep it was almost dawn. Hinton woke up just minutes before Millie. He did not want to disturb her and so without moving he stared at the reproduction of the Paul Gauguin painting on the wall. At first he wondered about the choice of the artwork. He had seen the original of Two Tahitian Women in the Metropolitan Museum of Art in New York where it was part of their permanent exhibit. Oh well, it was a famous piece. Then he saw it and he could have kicked himself for having missed the tiny camera during his search of the room. The right eye of the partially nude woman in the painting had been replaced with the camera. Could he have been distracted by the beauty of the woman or her nudity when he was searching for cameras and microphones? Stupid but possible. Now he hoped that Johnston, the mystery woman or whoever placed the camera was enjoying the less than x-rated show they had put on last night. Whoever it was would learn very little from watching it. They had talked about many things and consumed a fairly large quantity of wine but there was no show, and nothing said to give anyone information on what Hinton or Millie was up to.

When Millie woke up shortly after this discovery, Hinton did not mention the camera or their new roles as movie stars. He would tell her after they left the hotel. Millie was not ready to leave the hotel room. But soon, Hinton insisted that they get something to eat and see at least a little of this magnificent city. It was too late for breakfast in the hotel restaurant, but they managed to order some croissants, fruit, and a couple of espressos.

From Gare du Nord, it was only a few minutes and one change of trains at Gare de L'est to Place de la Concorde, made famous during the French revolution for the executions of Louis XVI and Marie Antoinette. From there, they walked to Champs-Élysées, past the Louvre, and at least close to the Arc de Triomphe. They walked down the other side of Champs-Élysées and they eventually ended up at Pont Neuf, where Hinton knew they could catch a ride on one of the tourist boats. The river was dirty, the boat was full of tourists, but the views were spectacular.

When the river tour was finished, it was only a short walk to the left bank and cafe Les Deux Magots, where Hemingway, Gertrude Stein and other intellectuals engaged in various intrigues in the 1920s and 1930s. It was the one place Millie had mentioned that she wanted to see. The Café was now simply a tourist trap and like thousands before them they sat down outside and had a glass of over-priced, mediocre red wine. Hinton took this opportunity to tell Millie about the camera in their room. After her initial outrage, Millie smiled and said: "Let's give them an even better show this evening. I am not an exhibitionist, but I don't really care. If they want to watch, let them watch. We could even give them some false information about Ross and the murders. They would waste a lot of time sorting that out." They had an early dinner at *Le Café des Beaux Arts*, hardly a culinary delight, but the atmosphere was pleasant, and the service displayed the unhurried amiable inefficiency of many French restaurants. The food was at least decent. Even the table wine was better than the expensive vinegar they drank earlier at *Deux Magots*. Millie loved the tour but was a little disappointed that they had skipped the Louvre and a chance to see the Mona Lisa. Hinton had explained that the lines were so long it would take hours to see the Mona Lisa. He told Millie that Mona Lisa Lost Her Smile. Millie grinned and laughed a bit at the reference to David Allan Coe's famous song. She then said, "You can take the boy out of Texas, but you can't take Texas out of the boy." Hinton was pleased with himself for showing the expertise of a local guide, but it had been a long day with little sleep and the old friends headed back to the hotel.

During their excursion, Hinton watched carefully for familiar faces or any indication that they were being followed. He noticed nothing but he also knew that well-trained professionals could follow them without being observed. Since they were on the left bank, they took the metro from the Saint Michel station. They did not need to change trains and in only a few minutes they were back at Gare du Nord.

The hotel had been cleverly designed so that it was not possible to reach the elevators without passing the restaurant and the bar. As they approached the bar, Hinton looked at Millie with a frown on his face. She too had recognized Chuck Johnston sitting in the bar with a glass of wine. They could have pretended not to see Johnston, but that would only delay the process, so they sat down uninvited at his table.

Hinton began the conversation, "Why the hell am I worth all this attention? Couldn't you just leave us alone for a while to enjoy Paris?" Hinton did not bother to ask how Johnston had found them.

Johnston's explanation was less than satisfactory. "We want you to find Ross, we want the murders solved, and we want to know what is going on with the new energy policy from the Saudis. Besides, you are a player in the energy game whether you like it or not. You know oil industry executives around the world. You know the Saudis, Russians, Nigerians, and others. They listen to you, as we do. Your words make an impact. You have influence. That makes you a valuable player. We can't ignore you."

Hinton was skeptical, "I have about as much influence with the industry as a half-pint of whiskey split eight ways in a Texas deer hunting camp. I'm an academic researcher who finds the industry to be a fascinating topic. I am not a player. You must have a reason for being here so tell us what you know and don't be uncomfortable talking in front of Millie. She knows everything I know – maybe more than I know."

Johnston began by explaining that British Customs had identified Ross boarding a plane for Vienna. "We asked them not to detain him even though London police wanted to question him about the murder of Dianne Stoddard. We assured the British authorities that we would keep close tabs on him but our agent who was on the same flight lost him at the airport. Ross was sitting near the front of the plane. Our agent was in the back. Ross got off the plane first. We are not sure that Ross took any evasive action or even knew he was being followed. Our facial recognition software found a match on the photos of the mystery woman from the photos you got from the Hotel Tavistock. We also found a match of the images you sent yesterday with the London photos. The woman in Paris is obviously younger looking but either she is young and previously disguised herself as older or vice versa. The problem is that the so-called match is with a woman in Calgary. The matched woman is the assistant manager of a large hotel in Calgary. We are reasonably certain that she was not in DC, London, or Paris on the days you encountered her. She has no siblings. We have checked cousins with no success. It is possible that one or the other of this woman's parents had a secret child but there is no evidence to support that idea. She remains the mystery woman."

Hinton thought the Agency was incompetent and was tempted to say so. Instead, he said, "Calgary is a fun city. Among other things it is also an oil town. Have you checked to see if she has some connection to the industry? Someone could have covered for her at the hotel while she traveled."

Hinton didn't buy any of this story, and Johnston still denied that the woman was an Agency employee or contract worker.

Millie broke the awkward silence. "There has been little or no progress since that Friday afternoon in Norman. The whole thing is preposterous. Two women are dead, an economist is sort of missing, another economist is trying to find the first one, there's a mystery woman that no one can identify or claim as their own, there is intrigue about Saudi energy policy, and the resources of more than one intelligence agency are of no apparent use. Ross could have killed the women. The mystery woman could have killed the women. Chuck Johnston, at the moment having a glass of French wine in Paris, could have killed the women. Someone not even on the list could have killed the women, or maybe the murders are not even related. You couldn't sell this story to a bunch of drunks in a Texas honky tonk at closing time. You two can sit here and speculate all you want. I'm going to bed."

Hinton followed Millie to the room, leaving Johnston to finish his wine or do whatever he was going to do. On the way to the room Millie observed that there had been no mention of the camera in the room. Hinton said he had seen no point in mentioning it. Johnston would have denied any knowledge of it even if he had placed it there himself.

When they entered the room, Hinton took off his shirt and casually tossed it toward the painting. This maneuver could not have been better. The shirt caught on the top of the painting and covered the camera. Millie grinned.

They turned out the lights and got in the bed. The two old friends were soon asleep. Nothing happened that would have interested the owner of the camera.

Chapter 7

Vienna

The next morning, Hinton insisted on going with Millie to the airport. Millie had deliberately picked a flight departing from Orly Airport rather than the much busier Charles de Gaulle Airport. Orly was also closer, only ten miles south of Paris, and easily reached by train. They did not talk much on the way to the airport. Both knew that their relationship had changed completely. No, they had not had sex but there was something very different emotionally in their relationship that could not be ignored. Yet neither one wanted to talk about what their new relationship might or might not be. They would not even have a relationship if Hinton was dumb enough to get himself killed chasing Ross, solving murders, and perhaps trying to alter world energy markets.

All too soon, it was time for Millie to check in and go through customs. There were only a few others in line at the American Airlines counter. Briefly, Hinton thought how easy it would be to buy a ticket and return to Oklahoma with Millie, but he was looking forward to dinner with the Rabbi and Shabazz in Vienna and he was always fascinated by the OPEC meetings. Maybe he would also find Ross. No, abandoning his plans was not an option.

Hinton waited until Millie walked through the security gate without so much as a goodbye kiss. Suddenly, the thought of a twelve-hour train ride to Vienna was not very appealing. Besides, a little unplanned quasi-random behavior was probably a good safety move. Unless someone had followed them to Orly, no one would know of his travel itinerary. So Hinton walked over to a RyanAir counter and bought a ticket on a flight to Vienna leaving in about an hour. He canceled his train reservation, bought a cup of coffee and a croissant, and felt very pleased with himself. His hotel reservation in Vienna was not until the next night but he knew he could find some place to stay even in a city crowded with OPEC participants, reporters, and gawkers.

The two-hour flight to Vienna was uneventful and on-time. The Vienna Airport, located in Schwechat, was only ten or twelve miles from downtown. Hinton was waived through customs since his flight was from another EU country. The airport was modern, clean, and almost sterile but you could catch the train to downtown directly from the terminal. The main railway station in Vienna, *Wien Hauptbahnhof*, built in 2012 was also clean and modern.

First things first; Hinton needed to find a hotel. The *Wien Hauptbahnhof* Hotel, part of the a&o chain, was just behind the station. They had several rooms available, and Hinton selected one with a view. Just like the train station it was named after, the hotel was immaculately clean, almost too clean for Hinton, who preferred older hotels with a little character. He canceled the hotel reservation that Millie made for him for the next night. By now, Hinton was hungry. The hotel had a snack bar with a limited menu. Hinton wandered outside and soon found Sichuan Restaurant. Who would expect that you would find great Chinese food in Vienna?

After the dinner, Hinton sent a text to the Rabbi telling him the name of his hotel. They also confirmed a dinner on Tuesday night with Shabazz. Within an hour, a courier arrived with a small package containing OPEC+ credentials for the meeting scheduled to start on Thursday. Hinton would have nearly two days to himself. He knew exactly what to do with the extra time.

The International Institute for Applied Systems Analysis (IIASA) was in the small, beautiful town of Laxenburg, only about 15 miles from Vienna's main railway station and the hotel where he was staying. There was good bus service from the railway station to Laxenburg. IIASA was in *Schloss Laxenburg*, a famous castle where, among others, the last emperor of Austria, Franz Joseph, spent summers. Hinton decided to visit IIASA in the morning. He knew that Jurgen Hausman, an old friend and energy expert, was temporarily at IIASA.

Jurgen greeted Hinton warmly and the two men updated each other on their recent activities. Jurgen began the conversation, "For more than two years I have been the executive director of the Climate and Energy Consortium. I came to Laxenburg to make certain that I was up to date on the latest model evaluation techniques. The Consortium has offices in London, Berlin, DC, Rio, New Delhi, and Cairo. The Consortium employs nearly 200 scientists, engineers, and policy experts. We hired climate scientists, petroleum engineers, geologists, biologists, economists, political scientists, and people from a host of other fields. The Consortium is funded by the governments of Saudi Arabia, the Russian Federation, Australia, Japan, Korea, a few other nations, and most of the major multi-national energy firms."

"The Consortium's mission is to provide an independent assessment of the UN's International Panel on Climate Change (IPCC) reports and recommendations. The IPCC had warned of catastrophic increases in temperature (more than 1.5 degrees centigrade by the end of the century) if the world did not reverse current trends on carbon emissions by 2030. The movement promoting net zero by 2050 was a direct outgrowth of recent IPCC reports. I have had a lot of fun being the executive director and the work is important."

Hinton interjected, "I am aware of the Consortium, but I dismissed it as an effort by oil producers to discredit the IPCC and its reports. To be honest, I was surprised that you, a man of considerable academic integrity, is a part of it."

Not surprised at all by Hinton's remarks, Jurgen responded, "I hear that a lot, but that kind of criticism is unfair. That was my reaction when I was first approached to become part of the team. But then I learned that the group had insisted on complete independence and no interference in their work. This is a legitimate effort. Our first report will be released in a month or so and it will be a bombshell. The IPCC was too cautious. They did not go far enough. To avoid cataclysmic climate changes, the world needs to end all fossil fuel production by 2040. Net zero by 2050 is not enough. Even ending fossil fuel production by 2040, will still leave the world to face the unpleasant consequences of the damage already done for several decades. "

Hinton's smile indicated approval and he said so to Jurgen. "I am glad you have not sold your soul to the devil, and I look forward to reading your report. The world is in a truly precarious situation, but I am always torn in two directions on this issue. There is no doubt that most of the world's population enjoyed much higher living standards because of fossil fuels over the last century. Imagine living without cars and trucks or airplanes to carry us almost anywhere in the world in a matter of hours. Ocean transportation would still be sailing ships. Oh well, we can talk more about that over a beer or two. If I remember correctly, there is a beer garden close by."

With more enthusiasm than was normal for Jurgen, he said, "Let's go. It is a perfect day for some cold beer and good conversation."

As the two men walked to the beer garden, Hinton changed the topic, "Have you seen Doug Ross? He is not answering his phone and he has not responded to my emails. We were scheduled to have dinner in London, but I have not heard from him. I thought he might have been in touch with you."

Jurgen stopped walking and with a puzzled look on his face responded, "Funny you should ask. Lowell Smith-Thompson called me a few days ago and asked about Ross. He said Ross was supposed to appear at a roundtable discussion at LSE last week but did not show up. Lloyd knew that Ross was also scheduled to give a seminar here and he wanted to know if Ross had canceled. Ross has not cancelled, and I expect him to be here tomorrow at 10 am for the seminar. I have never heard of Ross being a no-show for anything, but he has not responded to my emails or phone calls either. Very strange behavior."

"Can I come to the seminar tomorrow? I would really like to find Ross."

"Of course. The seminar is open to the public and it would be nice to have you there as well."

Hinton did not want to press the issue about Ross. There was no need to tell Jurgen that Ross was his main purpose for visiting or that Ross was wanted for questioning by police in both DC and London. That would do no one any good. In any case, Hinton and Jurgen had other things to talk about. The two spent almost three hours discussing the latest developments in energy modeling and energy policy. They did so without neglecting their real purpose, which was to consume large quantities of beer. They did this with enthusiasm, sampling as many different beers as they could. Finally, Hinton ended this seminar by telling Jurgen that he had an important dinner date in Vienna in only a few hours. In fact, the dinner was scheduled for the next night, but Hinton had consumed enough beer.

Hinton slept well in the sterile atmosphere of his hotel. Just before 9 am, he walked into Jurgen's office at IIASA. Chuck Johnston, who had been informed by Hinton of Ross's seminar, was already there and engaged in a lively conversation about the Green economy with Jurgen. Apparently, the two had hit it off well even after Johnston had told Jurgen who he was and what he was doing in Vienna. Hinton joined the conversation but, in fact, said very little. He had learned long ago how to carry on a conversation in a very articulate fashion without saying much of anything. Ross was not mentioned but it was obvious that the three men were just passing time waiting on his arrival.

A few minutes later a cheerful and unusually confident Ross came through the door. Hinton lightly reprimanded Ross for not returning his emails or phone calls and then introduced Johnston, who got right to the point.

"The police in DC and London would like to talk to you about the deaths of Patti Walker and Diane Stoddard. Apparently, you were among the last people to see either one of them. You were in the right places at the right time to commit both murders. The difficulty of finding you adds to their desire to interview you. The Agency also thinks you are a prime suspect. What's going on?"

Ross did not seem surprised or disturbed by Johnston's accusations. Very calmly, Ross replied,

"I know what it might look like, but I did not kill these two women. Yes, I knew both of them and yes, I was with them shortly before they were killed, but as I said, I did not do it. As for my absence in recent days, I just wanted some time to myself while I contemplated my own version of a middle-age crisis. Besides, I would hardly be giving a public presentation this morning if I wanted to evade anyone."

Johnston was not convinced but he did consider the possibility that Ross was telling the truth. He had no legal authority to detain Ross. He could have informed the local police that a man wanted for questioning in London and DC about two murders was in Laxenburg but he decided that Ross would provide little or no new information no matter who did the questioning. There was no point in continuing and he turned to Jurgen, who was obviously a bit anxious about the start of the seminar in just a few minutes.

Jurgen took the opportunity to intervene. "We have moved the seminar to a larger room down the hall. The posters or recent press attention to the industry generated a larger than expected crowd. The small seminar room will no longer do. The event has also attracted some press types who want to question the three of us after the seminar. Without permission, I agreed."

The seminar Ross presented was not exactly exciting, but it did go well, and the audience gave a good round of applause when it was over. Ross's main thesis was that the oil and gas industry was undergoing the most rapid changes in its history. The changes were more than the widely known technological changes – fracking and horizontal drilling. There was, Ross contended, the most profound structural change within the industry since the Rockefellers tried to monopolize it more than 100 years ago. Add climate change and geopolitical instability to the mix and you might not be able to recognize the industry just a few years from now. Ross was not finished. He argued that the age of fossil fuels will end sooner than anyone in the room thinks. He declared it is over.

The Q&A session was lively and after the general audience left, the press wanted more but Ross either knew nothing more or would not give them what they wanted.

Johnston offered Hinton a ride back to Vienna. Ross was going to spend a couple of days with Jurgen. That was fine with Hinton and as soon as they were in the car, he told Johnston that his assignment was complete, mission accomplished, and that he would return to being the academic that he really was.

Johnston replied, "Yes, we can now keep tabs on Ross. We don't know if he did the murders or not. We don't know if he is involved in something larger, but we can watch him carefully. We appreciate your help in finding him. There are other things you should know. Cindy Burgess is alive and well. She was seen in London with Ross and we lost her, fearing the worst. But we have now interviewed her. She said Ross was the perfect gentleman when they were together. He understood completely and did not protest when she left to go spend a night or two with her lover, apparently another woman. We have provided security for her. No one cares who she sleeps with."

Johnston continued, "Your mystery woman was given OPEC press credentials yesterday with the name, Marie Churchill. We assume that the name is false. We find no record of a journalist by that name or anyone using that name. You should also know that this woman, whoever she is, spent an hour with your friend Rabbani before she picked up her press credentials. She has vanished once again. Before we could get anyone in place to follow her, she just disappeared. She might be the most dangerous person in this little game. Since she made a habit of following you or at least showing up where you happened to be on several occasions, she could also be a threat to you. If you are returning home, Deuce and the Director would be very grateful if you stopped by Langley during your trip home."

When Johnston dropped Hinton at his hotel, his last words were "See you soon."

Hinton did not trust Johnston and he thought this feeling was probably mutual. Johnston could be lying or telling something less than the whole truth on any number of issues. What Hinton looked forward to was dinner with the Rabbi and Shabazz. He would deal with Johnston later.

Hinton arrived fashionably late at the address given to him by the Rabbi, but he was a bit taken back by the absence of any signage on the building. Hinton reached for the doorbell but before he was able to touch it, a large well-dressed man opened the door and said: "Yes, Professor Hinton you are in the right place. Dr. Rabbani and his wife are waiting for you. Please come in."

The restaurant was not a restaurant at all but rather one of seven private residences owned by the Saudi Embassy in Vienna. For security purposes, the residences were bought and sold frequently. Any given residence might be used only for a few months. Often, the Saudis made money on these real estate transactions. The Saudis were not alone in engaging in this quasi-clandestine procedure. The Russian, British, French, and American embassy delegations engaged in similar practices. Sometimes they even traded properties among themselves.

Shabazz and the Rabbi greeted Hinton warmly and the three of them spent nearly an hour discussing family status, old friends, and plans and hopes for the future. With smiles all around, Shabazz even referred to Hinton's graduate school crush on her. As always, they discussed how their lives might have been different If Hinton and not the Rabbi had managed to marry Shabazz. None of them had any regrets about the way things turned out. World affairs, politics, and the oil industry were not mentioned in the pre-dinner conversation.

The meal was delicious. Shabazz had declined the offer of one of the embassy chefs to prepare the meal. She took it upon herself to prepare Kabsa as the main dish. Kabsa is a traditional Saudi dish, similar in some respects to chicken biryani which is now served from the Middle East to India with regional and local variations. The Saudi twist on

Kabsa is that the meat used to prepare the meal is not necessarily chicken. A fresh green salad and Saudi cookies called *ma'amoul* completed the meal. The dinner conversation was also light and cheerful. The Rabbi could not resist mentioning that Shabazz had cooked this meal for Hinton on their one and only so-called date.

Hinton and the Rabbi cleared the dishes from the table and the three adjourned to the living room to continue the conversation which turned serious in a hurry. The Rabbi began the talk but this time there was no smile on his face.

"About two hours ago, two Saudi energy facilities were attacked by drones. The facilities at Khurais and Abquiq produce about 8.5 million barrels of oil per day. You know where they are – just north and east of Riyadh. It is likely that more than half of the Kingdom's oil production, as much as 5 or 6 million barrels per day, will be off-line for some time but we have only very preliminary estimates of the damage. The fires from the explosions are still burning. Smoke can be seen from 50 to 60 miles away. No deaths have been reported."

"Yemeni Houthis are taking credit for the attacks, claiming they used ten drones. Our intelligence services and the Crown Prince think it is unlikely that the Houthis could pull this off on their own. There is even a question about whether the attacks came from Yemen or Iraq or even Iran. As you know, the Kingdom, with the backing of the UAE and quieter backing from your own government, has been attacking the Houthi rebels for several years. Sometimes US warplanes and drones are used in the attacks on the Houthis. The Houthis truly are a threat to our national security but no amount of bombing the Houthis will defeat them. They ruled most of what is now called Yemen for thousands of years. They will not give up easily."

The Rabbi continued. "The press knows about the attack, and it is or

78

will be front-page news almost everywhere. The media pundits and so-called experts are busy speculating on how high oil prices will go. They can speculate all they want and one or two of them may even be correct. The press does not yet know what I am about to tell you and I am only telling you because of our long-standing friendship."

Without giving Hinton a chance to react, the Rabbi pressed on. "First, the OPEC+ meetings, scheduled to begin in about 36 hours, will be canceled early tomorrow morning. There will be no announcements about a change in Saudi energy policy. No production quotas will be reached. The price of oil will be very high for the next few weeks without any agreement that might have been reached at the meetings. Shabazz and I along with most members of the Saudi delegation will return to Riyadh shortly after tomorrow's cancellation announcement."

Other than a strange look on his face, Hinton still did not react.

"My friend," the Rabbi continued, "Now would be the perfect time for you to visit the Kingdom. In the past you have always had an excuse for not visiting, but if you truly want to understand the oil industry, you must come to Saudi Arabia and see it for yourself. Shabazz and I have the Learjet at our disposal. We can fly you to Riyadh, make sure you get to see the things you need to see, and return you to Vienna. We will leave tomorrow morning. Will you come with us?"

Hinton thanked his friend the Rabbi and quickly accepted the offer. For the next few minutes the conversation returned to old times and took on a much lighter tone. All too soon, Hinton knew it was time to leave.

Hinton walked back to the hotel. On foot, this was about a forty-five-minute journey. He needed the time to decompress from a long day and relax a bit before he went to Riyadh.

Chapter 8
Riyadh

Hinton looked forward to spending more time with the Rabbi and Shabazz. Even more he looked forward to time without Ross, Johnston, and the mystery woman. He had had enough of that. As promised, the Rabbi and Shabazz arrived at the hotel lobby at 9 am in a Chevrolet Suburban, which seems to be the vehicle of choice these days for diplomats and drug dealers. Hinton had to admit that it was a very comfortable vehicle, plenty of room, and it had all the extras. He wondered if he could ever give up his jeep for one of these, and he was glad he did not need to decide this morning.

The ride to the airport was about twenty minutes. They pulled up to a gate leading to the general aviation area. The guard at the gate looked at the driver's badge and waived them through. They drove right up to the Learjet and were greeted by an Austrian customs officer who stamped their passports as having left the EU. There was no other security to get through and they boarded the plane. The pilot greeted the Rabbi warmly and nodded pleasantly to the rest of us. The pilot said that the flight time was approximately eight hours, that the weather was good, and that we would stop briefly in Istanbul to refuel. The tower gave us clearance and we were off.

A Learjet is a marvelous machine, very comfortable and very fast. Long ago Hinton had decided that if he were filthy rich, he would always fly first class. Now, he asked himself if he could change his mind. Flying in your own private jet was much better than any first-class ticket on any airline. Oh well, he was not filthy rich and so he should just sit back and enjoy this flight.

Soon after take-off, Hinton, the Rabbi, and Shabazz were deep in conversation as old friends should be. They talked about everything. They talked about the Learjet which was no big deal to the Rabbi or Shabazz. They talked about old times in Austin and how they would have changed the graduate programs at UT if they had been in charge. They talked about the two Rabbani kids and Leslie. They talked about world political and possible military crises and the general uncertainty of living in the twenty-first century. They talked about oil markets. They talked about sports, but Hinton was at a disadvantage when it came to soccer. He simply did not know the game as well as the Rabbi or Shabazz. At no point in the discussion was there a topic on which Shabazz or the Rabbi were not well-informed. Only two subjects seemed off-limits. They did not discuss the Royal Family or Linda. No one had to set the rules. They simply knew not to do this.

After some snacks and a couple of non-alcoholic drinks, the conversation turned to Saudi Arabia, or the Kingdom as the Rabbi and Shabazz referred to it. The Rabbi talked enthusiastically about Vision 2030, the Saudi development plan for the next generation. Shabazz and the Rabbi agreed that the plan would transform the Kingdom into a nation most of the world would envy. Modernization was not an easy task, but the Kingdom was the only nation with the financial and other resources to pull it off. Whenever Hinton expressed any doubt, Shabazz and the Rabbi very politely said: "Keep your skepticism bottled up until you see with your own eyes what is already taking place."

Eventually, Hinton mentioned the State Department travel advisory urging US Citizens to travel to some other place than Saudi Arabia. The advisory was a level 4 advisory, one of the strongest issued by State. The Rabbi said that Hinton was probably as safe in the Kingdom as in the US. He pointed out that more than forty thousand people were killed by gunfire in the US during the past year. This was the start of a conversation that lasted a while and helped the long flight seem like a short one. The Rabbi mentioned that both Patti Walker and Diane Stoddard had contributed in major ways to the Vision 2030 plan. Now, both are dead, he said. The Rabbi pointed out that it is a dangerous game we play. We must all take precautions to be safe.

Hinton commented, "No one is safe from a determined professional killer. You might be able to keep the Crown Prince safe but only if he is safe from his own family members."

The Rabbi replied, "You may be right, but Shabazz and I are delighted that you are finally visiting our country. We will keep you safe and you will have the opportunity to see first-hand the dual nature of our society and the dilemma faced by the Royal Family."

Hinton nodded, "You taught me long ago that the Kingdom is shaped by two major forces: History and tradition on one hand and the quest for modernization and development on the other."

"Yes, you will recall from my history lessons that the Royal family owes its existence to Wahhabism. In the middle of the 18th Century, what is now Saudi Arabia was just a bunch of nomadic tribes wandering around the peninsula. Then, in 1745 Muhhamad bin Saud, our first king, made a deal with Muhhamud Wahhab, an Islamic cleric. Wahhab would provide religious justification for Saud to unify the tribes. Wahhab was a fundamentalist who advocated strict adherence to the teachings of the Prophet including *Sharia* law. Wahhabism is still with us today and some Wahhabis went to fight with the Islamic State in Iraq and Syria."

Hinton frowned and asked, "Can Wahhabism be eliminated?"

"No. But before his death King Abdullah banned some of the more egregious Wahhabi practices such as public floggings and beheading criminals. The floggings still go on in dark streets and remote areas, but they are not condoned by the Saudi government. Within the last few years, the Crown Prince declared that women no longer must wear the *Hijab* when in public and women may now drive, but there is still a long way to go. The Wahhabis are the greatest internal threat. Some of the younger, more rabid members of the group think acts of violence, terror if you prefer, are okay to further their goals."

"And this goes on in parallel with the ambitious modernization plans of Vision 2030?"

"Absolutely. And we have external threats as well. The Houthi's in Yemen are a constant source of acts of terror. They were probably responsible for the refinery attacks."

"Yes, I know, and you use the F16s and F22s we sold you to retaliate. That won't do you any good. It will just make them angrier and more bitter. Better to strike a deal with the Houthis."

"Easier said than done, and we have other external issues as well. For the most part, we are Sunni Muslims while our neighbors Iran and Iraq are Shiites. We have avoided war with Iran and Iraq, thanks in large part to our overwhelming air superiority. They don't want to take us on and we were not disappointed that they spent a decade fighting each other. Generally, we get along with the UAE states. Qatar, however, has been a problem, especially after they decided to recognize Israel. In any case, we think there is hope for a stable Middle East."

"Good luck with that. I hope you are right, but I just don't see stability in your future. You also have a problem with Syria and their friends, the Russians. I understand why you brought the Russians into OPEC+, but don't trust them for a second. They will mess with you at the first opportunity. Tell me about the other side of the coin – modernization."

"The Kingdom already has a lot of modern aspects to it. A good example is King Abdullah University of Science and Technology (KAUST) where I did my first year of undergraduate work. Modernization really began just after World War II. Riyadh back then was just a small village. It is now home to more than five million Saudis and a few foreigners. As you will see, Riyadh is a modern city with skyscrapers and well-designed streets and transportation. It is a comfortable place to live but it will be dwarfed by The Line."

"I want to go see what has been done on The Line, even though I know that you have just begun excavating. The idea of building a city from scratch that is 170 km long and only 0.2 Km wide that will be home to 9 million people by 2030 is like something out of a science fiction novel. Add to that your Vision 2030 plan says there will be no cars and the entire city will be carbon free. The plan claims you will be able to get from one end of The Line to the other in twenty minutes. Incredible. And it will have universities, schools, opera houses, movie theaters, and be close to nature. I need to see this, even if all that is there is a big ditch."

"We will see that you get there. It may be a bit difficult, but it can be arranged. We are also building resorts and many other attractions in the area that you must see to believe. We think this will change urban architecture and urban planning for the rest of the century. We want people from all over the world to come see it and take our concepts for urban living with them."

"This sounds like a utopia. Others who have attempted to build the ideal world have failed and you have many obstacles to overcome, and they are not just engineering and construction obstacles. Does the Royal Family understand that this will require further social reforms including freedom of the press, freedom of religion, and genuinely democratic institutions?"

"The Crown Prince and his family are fully committed to the project. The Saudi government will spend $200 billion or so on The Line and another $300 billion on other projects in the region. They know what they are doing. Just wait and see. There are other amazing things on the horizon and that is why we will announce a transition to a carbon free world and a major reduction in oil output as soon as conditions seem right."

A skeptical Hinton asked, "What else have you done with your magic wand?"

"We have not announced it yet, but we have discovered large deposits of lithium, the critical ingredient for EV batteries. We don't have cobalt, copper, or nickel or at least we have not found them yet, but we are securing supplies. We have just begun construction on a large lithium mine 75 kilometers south of Riyadh. Near the lithium mine we are building a battery factory that in two years will be capable of producing batteries for a million cars and light trucks per year. In two or three years, we plan to be producing batteries that do not require cobalt or nickel. We already have large stakes in companies developing lithium batteries with sulfur dioxide and others that will use a sodium solution. We are building an EV factory nearby and it will produce vehicles for both domestic consumption and export. We have the expertise to do this. We have been investing in EV manufacturers around the world for several years. We have already hired some of the best automotive engineers in the world to help us design the factory. It will work. We can show you the lithium mine if you want, but at this point it is mainly a big hole in the ground."

"You sound like a member of the Saudi Chamber of Commerce.

Are you being told to say this, or do you really think it might work?"

"I would not lie to you. You once told me that an advantage of growing up in Texas was that you could smell horseshit from a mile away."

"Okay but tell me about oil and gas. According to Baker-Hughes, you only have thirty-five or forty active rigs at any given time, and you are producing ten or twelve million barrels a day. In the US we have ten times that many rigs operating in the Permian alone and twenty times that many active rigs in the US not counting offshore rigs. How do you pull that off?"

"For the most part, we don't need to frack or drill horizontally for oil. The geology is different. When you frack a well in the US, initial production comes in at a thousand or twelve hundred barrels per day and then production declines sharply over the next several months. In a year that well may be only producing two-hundred barrels a day. That means you must keep drilling to keep up production. Our wells last for years before we see any significant decline in production. So we just don't need to drill as much as you do. This also gives us a significant cost savings over the US."

"So tell me about natural gas in the Kingdom."

"We do not export or import natural gas. Domestic consumption of natural gas is all covered by domestic production. We have a problem here. We are still generating most of our electricity from oil and that is not a smart thing to do. We have been slowly increasing the amount of electricity generated from natural gas and we have plans to increase that even further. Most of the gas we produce now is associated gas – gas that we get as a byproduct of producing oil. That will change. Our goal under the Vision 2030 plan is to produce nearly all electricity by natural gas or renewables."

"How are you going to increase natural gas production that much?"

"We have huge shale gas reserves, especially in the Jafurah fields. We estimate that there is more than 300 trillion cubic feet of natural gas there alone. That will require fracking and our plan calls for a hundred billion dollars of investment to make it work. We have plenty of sand for fracking – even plenty of good sand. We have the chemicals needed. Water for fracking is an issue but we will overcome that. Our biggest challenge is that we don't have the pipelines and infrastructure in place to generate all of our electricity by natural gas."

"This sounds like another very ambitious plan, and the Kingdom seems to have a lot of things going on simultaneously. Good luck with that. I'll come back in 2030 and see how you have done."

When the Rabbi got up to use the facilities, Shabazz leaned over and said: "I have arranged a surprise birthday party for Rabbani. He hates surprises and does not like parties, but it is his fiftieth birthday, and I will give him no choice. The party will be in a room at your hotel, The Intercontinental, on Saturday afternoon. So please keep Saturday afternoon open – no matter what he tries to arrange for you."

Hinton told Shabazz that he would do that, but he had no birthday gifts for the Rabbi. Shabazz said: "You are gift enough. You can't imagine what it means to the Rabbi to have you here."

When the plane arrived in Riyadh, they quickly went through customs formalities and the Rabbi and Shabazz dropped him off at the Intercontinental Hotel. The Rabbi apologized for dumping him in a hotel. The problem was that part of their very large home was being remodeled. He also told Hinton that he had to work tomorrow, but that a petroleum engineer named Abdul Hassan would pick him up at 7 am to take him on a tour of some nearby oilfields. Arrangements for visiting a refinery, the lithium mine, and the line would also be made. The Rabbi told Hinton that he would like Abdul.

The hotel was a splendid place with swimming pools, well-kept gardens, and walking paths. Overall, the place had the feel of a resort appropriate for Hawaii, Miami, or Bali. Hinton ate a fine meal in one of several restaurants at the hotel and went to bed early.

At 7 am on Thursday, Abdul was waiting for him in the lobby and greeted him with a single word: "Boomer."

Hinton responded with the expected "Sooner" that anyone affiliated with OU would know to say.

"Professor Hinton, our paths have crossed before. When I was studying petroleum engineering at OU, you attended one of my classes."

"Abdul, just call me Eddie. No need for this ceremonial nonsense. We are both adults and professionals. I don't recall meeting you at OU."

"Okay, Eddie. I don't think we ever spoke but many of the students were impressed that an economist wanted to understand the technical details of the industry. Today, we are going to tour the Ghawar oilfields, about two hundred kilometers to the east and perhaps these fields will impress you even though this is not your first visit to an oilfield."

The ride seemed to take no time at all. Abdul and Hinton talked nonstop. Abdul worked for Saudi Aramco, the huge oil firm that drilled and operated the Ghawar oil fields, the largest producing conventional field in the world. Abdul was proud of his work and eager to show it to this visitor from his alma mater. Soon enough, they had arrived at the first rig. The shift supervisor had been told of their visit and he provided a thorough tour and was very responsive to all questions posed by Hinton or Abdul.

The rig was as modern as any Hinton had seen in the Permian. The rigs had all the latest gadgets including the ability to self-load pipe. The drill bits were designed by a firm in Pennsylvania specifically for the geology of this site. Unlike in years past, they rarely had to change a drill bit. They had all kinds of monitoring devices in the hole during drilling and for afterwards. They were especially sensitive to monitoring the pressure in the pool of oil. They did not want a new well to upset the pressure gradient elsewhere. They were drilling to a depth of 15,000 feet but could easily go deeper if they needed to.

Hinton asked about the last dry hole they had drilled. Both the supervisor and Abdul laughed. The supervisor said: "That doesn't happen much anymore but if you must know, it was November 2003. I was just the shift manager, not the operations manager as I am now. Some petroleum engineer told us to stop at 14,000 feet so we did. The petroleum engineer had miscalculated. A well about one kilometer away struck oil at 15,000 feet."

Abdul began to laugh more vigorously now. He had been the petroleum engineer who had made the miscalculation and had over-ridden a petroleum geologist. He thought he would lose his job over that one, but he did not.

They visited two more rigs that day and Hinton could hardly believe that he had seen nearly ten percent of the active rigs in Saudi Arabia. In the afternoon they went on a tour of the Saudi Aramco refinery on the outskirts of Riyadh. Hinton had been to refineries before and always found them to be the most complex part of the industry. This one was especially fascinating. It produced gasoline, jet fuel, propane, distillates, and special lubricants for both domestic consumption and export. What a trip. Hinton was exhausted at the end of the day. The Rabbi had been correct. He really liked Abdul.

Friday morning, Abdul was again waiting for Hinton in the lobby. "Eddie, today we are going to look at the lithium mine. I have not yet seen it, so I volunteered." Hinton was happy to have Abdul as his guide again. They seemed to understand each other. In a little more than an hour they were at the lithium mine. The mine was an impressive site—a mile long and two miles wide. The construction crews were working on removing twenty-five feet of topsoil and preparing stable roads into the hole. Next to the mine was a processing pit. They would need lots of water. The beginnings of the battery factory were less than a mile away and not far from that they were laying the foundation for the EV factory. These were massive facilities. Clearly, the Saudis were serious about this work.

On the way back to Riyadh, Abdul changed the topic, "While at OU, I became a huge fan of the football team. I knew nothing about American football, not even what a touchdown was, but I learned quickly. It is a fascinating game, almost like ballet. I really appreciate excellence, no matter where it is. How will the team do this year?"

"Two Heisman quarterbacks in a row would be hard to repeat. I think the team will be good but not what it has been the last couple of years. If you get to the US again, I can get you tickets. Part of my job is associated with athletics, and I know most of the coaches and many athletes."

"If you know so much about the team, please explain how they could lose to Kansas State at home."

Both laughed. No one could explain such a thing.

On Saturday morning, Hinton had requested some free time instead of a guided tour. He wanted to walk around Riyadh on his own and get a better feel for the city. That morning, he got up, ate breakfast in the hotel restaurant, bought a city map from the gift shop, and another cup of coffee. He sat down in the hotel lobby and began studying the map. He soon realized that except for picking out places to go, he did not need the map. Riyadh was laid out in a grid pattern with major streets every two kilometers. Combine that knowledge with the unmistakable landmarks of the giant twin towers and there was no need for a map.

When he looked up from the map, he saw the Rabbi approaching. The Rabbi walked directly to Hinton and wasted no time with pleasantries.

"Go pack your duffle bag and backpack. We are going on a trip. I will check you out while you are gone, but don't waste any time. I will explain in the car."

Hinton did as he was told. In less than five minutes, Hinton was at the front door, spotted the car, and tossed his bags in the back. When he got in, he asked the Rabbi where they were headed. In a calm but firm voice, the Rabbi explained,

"We are headed to the airport. The Learjet is fueled and ready. It will deliver you back to Vienna. You must leave the country at once. If you stay, I will not be able to protect you and your life will be in danger. For that matter, if you stay, my life may be in danger as well. You must go."

Hinton was floored, "What crimes have I allegedly committed? I have only been with your tour guides and in the hotel."

The Rabbi's face was stern as he replied, "About an hour ago, I was visited by an agent from the Security Service. I was told that you had committed crimes against the state. The particular crimes include treason and inciting insurrection against the Government of Saudi Arabia. The problem is in your social media posts and your blog titled Hinton's Hints on the Oil Industry. The issue is that in your most recent blog post you were critical of the Crown Prince, Mohammed bin Salmon. Under Saudi law, crimes against the state are punishable by long prison terms."

Hinton started to say something, but the Rabbi continued,

"Please don't interrupt. The Government does not like to conduct trials of foreigners. I have received word from the Crown Prince that if you are out of the country by noon today and the social media posts and blog are taken down, you will not be pursued or prosecuted. If you decide to stay, the most likely scenario is that your body will be found on the streets of Riyadh not far from your hotel. A miscreant with a long history of attacking and robbing foreigners will be arrested. A trial will be held. The miscreant will be convicted and given a long prison sentence. He will be taken in chains from the courtroom. In a few days he will quietly resume his duties with the security service. An alternative scenario is that you simply disappear, and your body is never found. It has happened before."

Hinton now had the chance to speak.

"Rabbi, I don't have any social media accounts and I do not have a blog. I just don't do anything like that. Surely your security service can confirm that. I have done nothing wrong."

The Rabbi's expression softened as he replied, "The true facts of the matter are not very important. The Government will simply not tolerate it whether you did this or not. The most recent blog was posted from the public computers in the business center of your hotel. I have seen printouts of the blog and some of your social media posts. You must leave. I can try to straighten this out later so that someday you might be able to return but for now, your visit is over."

Hinton's first thought was of the words from a Waylon Jennings song about good old boys: "I've been busted for things that I did and did not do." Hinton understood that he had no choice but to leave Riyadh and to do so now. The Rabbi delivered him to the plane on the tarmac and a customs agent stamped his passport. Hinton thanked the Rabbi and wished him a happy birthday. Within minutes the plane took off and the pilot told him they would simply reverse the route they had taken before.

With no one to talk to, the flight seemed to take much longer than before.

When the plane arrived in Vienna, the customs agent stamped his passport, and he was told that the car and driver would take him wherever he wanted to go in Vienna. Hinton asked the driver to take him to the main train station, where he got out, waited a minute or two and went inside the station and bought two tickets. The first was to the airport. At a second kiosk he bought a ticket to Paris. He then crossed the street to the Hotel Hauptbonhof, where he had stayed before. Hinton had not slept on the plane, and he was ready for some sleep. He thought he was safe enough even in a city that was home to many Saudis.

After checking in, Hinton called Johnston who did not answer. He knew that Johnston would eventually call him back and he didn't really want to talk with him anyway. Next Hinton called Millie and after a brief description of his trip, he asked for help from the fixer,

"Millie, I need some help. I had to leave Riyadh in a hurry. The Rabbi told me that social media accounts in my name as well as a blog had been very critical of the Crown Prince. In the Kingdom, that is treason, and I was given a very narrow window of time to leave the country or be arrested. Is there someone in IT who can remove this stuff from the internet?"

"I think I know just the right person in IT but it is Saturday. Do you happen to have passwords for any of the accounts?

"No Millie, they are not my accounts. You know what I think of social media. I'll call tomorrow to see what you have found out."

Part 2

People

Chapter 9

Ross

I was born in Midland, TX on July 5, 1972. I have always wanted to claim July 4th as my birthday so that I could celebrate my birthday and the nation's birthday on the same day. This is a trivial issue but one that has bothered me for as long as I can remember. As so many people have pointed out, you can't choose your birthday, your place of birth or your parents. If I could somehow do that, all three would be different choices.

Midland, and its inseparable twin city Odessa, is oil country. There is little to recommend in Midland or Odessa except oil and the money oil generates. Without oil, these two west Texas cities would probably be tiny little towns with only a feed store, a hardware store, gas stations, and a few other businesses serving the local ranches. But the oil is there. These two desolate places are in the Permian Basin – one of the most productive oil basins ever discovered. Oil has been produced in the Permian for nearly a century. Santa Rita Number 1 was an appropriate name for the gusher that came in on March 27, 1923. The name had been suggested by a Catholic priest in New York City who was advising two women not to invest in the well. Santa Rita is the patron saint of the impossible. Drilling the well encompassed all the intrigue, shaky finances, stubbornness, and risk long associated with wildcatters and the oil industry. The well had taken two years to drill to a depth of about 3,000 feet. A modern twenty-first century rig can drill four or five times that deep in just over a couple of weeks. Never mind the primitive technology. Never mind the fact that this was not the first well drilled in the Permian. Santa Rita was the first really successful well and it ushered in a century of booms and busts in the region and billions of dollars for the University of Texas trust fund. The University had been given a big chunk of seemingly worthless land in West Texas rather than cash by the Texas Legislature. Like thousands of other students, I would benefit from Santa Rita when I attended UT Austin. The original Santa Rita rig now sits on the UT Austin campus.

My grandfather, whom I never met, claimed to be a distant, perhaps very distant, relative of Ross Sterling, Governor of Texas from 1931 to 1933. He claimed that Governor Sterling's first name was a tribute to the Ross family. Some of this may or may not be true, but I have always claimed this relationship, and no one has ever challenged it.

Governor Sterling was a legend in the oil industry. Before becoming governor, he was a small-time driller and partner in a firm that eventually became Humble Oil, taken over by Standard Oil and now part of the Exxon Mobil group. Sterling's term as governor of Texas coincided with the worst days of the Great Depression and the incredible boom of the East Texas oil fields. No one had ever seen or even dreamed of such a giant oil field. Oil production was so high and demand so weak that the price of a barrel of oil fell to ten cents if you could find a buyer. Ten cents a barrel for oil was cheaper than a barrel of water or beer. Industry leaders knew there was a crisis on hand and the governor responded.

Under his emergency powers as governor, Sterling called out the National Guard and at gun point closed all 1,464 wells in East Texas. This action brought some relief to oil markets, but the important part of the story was that the Texas Legislature established the most successful oil cartel the industry has ever seen. This cartel made the feeble attempts of the Rockefellers to monopolize the industry in the late 19th and early

20th centuries look like the efforts of amateurs. More importantly, the Texas Cartel was not in violation of the Sherman Anti-trust Act.

At the time, most oil was shipped by rail. The great pipelines from East Texas to the East Coast had not yet been built. The most famous pipeline, known as the Big Ditch, running from Port Arthur to the East Coast was a product of WWII and the threats imposed by German submarines.

The State of Texas already had regulatory authority over railroads. The Legislature then gave the Texas Railroad Commission the authority to set daily allowable production limits. If you have control over production in the largest oilfield in the world, you also have control over the world price of oil. For nearly forty years, the Texas Railroad Commission used this power with considerable enthusiasm.

Texas was the oil capital of the world. It was without rivals until the late 1960s and early 1970s when OPEC became a major player. Legend has it that OPEC originated in Scholz's Garden, an Austin Texas beer garden – one of my favorite places. The University of Texas and its rival, the University of Oklahoma, had become the two premier institutions to learn petroleum geology. The sons but not many daughters of well-to-do Middle Easterners enrolled at these two institutions in large numbers. These good, almost always, Muslim students soon discovered the joys of drinking beer and other liquid refreshments at Scholz's. The Garden, as it was commonly called, was also a favorite drinking place of Texas Railroad Commission staffers and other government officials. Scholz's was a friendly place, and it was only natural that the students and staffers of the Railroad Commission would engage in conversation and share stories about what they did. The students, especially the Saudis, quickly learned that what the commission did was to control the world price of oil. It was no secret that the Middle

East contained a lot of oil. The students needed little instruction to reach the logical conclusion that they too could play the cartel game. When they returned home, they told their parents and OPEC was born. If there was a birth certificate for OPEC, place of birth would have been Scholz's Garden, Austin, Texas.

I learned the OPEC origination story from Eddie Hinton who had heard the story from some old-timers at Scholz's. Both of us have told the story many times and no one has ever bothered to challenge it. I owe Eddie a lot. Among other things, he helped me get through the comprehensive exams at UT, and he was instrumental in getting me the job at OU. I also resent him a great deal. I don't like being indebted to anyone and I don't like the fact that he has been more successful than I have been. It is too bad that we are not friends, but there is no real friendship between us.

I am getting ahead of my story about my connection to oil and gas. Both of my parents worked in the industry. My father was a crew chief, sometimes known as a site manager, on rigs for various exploration and production (E&Ps) firms. He was apparently very good at what he did. Making certain that a rig was operating 24/7 is no easy task. But there was something about him that meant he was always passed over for higher level management jobs. Maybe that explains his anger, bitterness, heavy drinking, and abusive behavior.

My mother was the director of human resources at a medium-sized oil field services firm. In boom times, the challenge she faced was to find qualified workers, which is no easy task. In the inevitable downturns in oil prices and drilling activity she faced a more difficult challenge. How do you layoff hard-working people you spent the previous two years doing everything you could to convince them that this was a great place to work? These workers always had families, mortgages, and auto loans.

Getting laid off is an intensely personal issue and often a life-crisis. So maybe it is not surprising that she too was bitter, angry, often drunk, and abusive. My childhood years were miserable.

We lived in a house built on 55 acres my parents had purchased at the top of one of the boom cycles. The house was just over nine miles west of Midland on land that no one thought about drilling. The fact that my parents had been unable to purchase the mineral rights to the property was a source of discontent, but not very important if there was no drilling. Nine miles may not seem like a long distance, but it might as well have been as far as New York City to my sister and me who had few friends because of the isolation.

The house was pretty much standard issue ranch-style. It had been expanded twice and is now about 2,500 square feet. A stand-alone three car garage had been added, connected to the house by a covered walkway. The only unusual feature of the house was that the original 1,500 square feet had a full basement. About half of it was used to store an accumulation of odds and ends and old furniture. The other half was a well-equipped tornado shelter. Midland is tornado country as well as oil country but not many people bothered to have a shelter.

Our shelter was elaborate and well-equipped. It had ventilation from the outside, a door to the outside, and double steel doors from the inside of the house. It was stocked with dry goods, canned goods, water, flashlights, and a first-aid kit. It was never used as a shelter, at least while I was there. Instead, that part of the basement was used as a whipping room.

I could not remember a time when I had not been spanked but by the time I was six or seven the spankings became whippings with a belt and then a variety of whips kept in the gun cabinet in the basement. Both of my parents engaged in this activity, sometimes together. Most of the time there was at least some pretense of some infraction of the rules I had committed. As I grew older, the whippings became more frequent and as often as not there was no reason given. My parents simply enjoyed whipping me. Later, I began to look forward to the whippings. The whippings terrified me, and the pain was real, but I enjoyed being tied up on the work bench in the basement and the anticipation of being whipped. On occasion, I did not hide the fact that I enjoyed it. Maybe they would quit if they thought I liked it. They did not quit but these strange feelings continue to the present day whenever I get the chance to be whipped.

When I was eleven, I discovered that my older sister, Phyllis, was also being whipped. Shortly after my discovery, I found her in her room stuffing some clothing and a few possessions into pillowcases. She had no suitcase. She told me that she was leaving and that her boyfriend was going to pick her up in a few minutes. Her last words to me before Joe arrived were "Get out of here as soon as you can." She moved into a trailer with Joe and a year later they had saved enough money to move to Dallas. As far as I know, she has never returned to the house. My parents did not seem to care that she left.

My ticket to freedom was baseball. By the time I was a freshman in high school, I was a pretty decent left-handed pitcher. My coach noticed my skills and also noticed that I was troubled. One day Coach told me that I could sharpen my baseball skills better if I lived closer to town. He said he lived in a large house with several extra rooms and that I was welcome to come stay with him during baseball season if I wanted. I jumped at the chance. For the rest of my high school years, I lived with Coach and his wife who became the only real parents I ever had. My own parents seemed happy to see me gone. They did not bother to come to games to watch me pitch.

By the time I was a senior in high school I had a baseball scholarship offer from Texas Tech. I accepted it immediately and I spent the next four years at Texas Tech. I was a decent left-handed pitcher but not the star I thought I would be. I did excel in the classroom, and I was offered a graduate assistantship in economics at UT Austin.

Graduate school was easy except for a couple of rough times. Other graduate students, especially Hinton, got me through the bad times. My live-in girlfriend was happy to indulge my whipping fantasies. Soon enough, I finished my doctoral program and embarked on an academic career. I had learned the formula for academic success. Publish a lot of journal articles that few people would read and obtain some research funding. The rest is easy and my job at OU gives me plenty of flexibility.

When Chuck Johnston questioned me in Vienna, I had an answer for everything he asked. I thought that if I satisfied Johnston, the police in DC and London would drop their investigations into my activities. Johnston asked me about Patti Walker. I told him that Patti gave me a ride from the party in Crystal City to the Wardman, where I picked up my car and went to Dulles. I told him that Patti was alive and well when I left her and that we had agreed to meet again when I returned from London.

Johnston then asked me about Diane Stoddard, and I told him that we had dinner and a nice conversation. I was sorry about her death, but I did not have anything to do with it. He then asked me about what I was doing with Cindy Burgess at the BDSM Society. I told him I had been given a guest card for one night and that we were both curious – voyeurs really. As soon as we left Cindy took off to be with her lover. I did not see her after that, but I was glad to hear that she is alive and well. What I did not tell him was that while we were there, Cindy gave me a thoroughly enjoyable whipping.

The last thing Johnston said to me was "Maybe you are innocent, I don't know. Hinton says you don't have the nerve to kill anyone or anything." Since this was not a question I did not respond. Instead, I told him that if he wanted to talk again, I would be available.

Hinton was wrong about me. Of course, I could kill. I already had killed. Occasionally it occurred to me that I should kill Hinton. Yes, he helped me get through graduate school. Yes, he got me the job at OU. But I have always resented his easy success and the fact that he is always one step ahead of me professionally.

I grew up shooting rabbits, rattlesnakes, javelina, and once I killed a coyote. I surprised the coyote and he had surprised me. He was staring at me when I pulled the trigger. Those big eyes haunted me for a long time. The coyote was no threat to me and was doing no harm. Most of the things we killed could be eaten. We would not eat the coyote. No more coyote hunting for me, but it would not be my last kill.

When I finished my degree at Texas Tech and headed for Austin and graduate school, I took a detour to Midland. Mainly, I wanted to say hello to Coach and tell him what I was up to. We had a great time, sharing stories and drinking a couple of beers. As I left his house, I decided to stop by my parent's home.

As soon as I opened the door, I knew it was a mistake. My mother was on the couch, passed out and her face and arms were badly bruised. A half-empty bottle of Vodka was also on the couch. My father was also passed out on the easy chair opposite the couch. He too had a few bruises and an open bottle in his lap. Without careful thought, I took the shotgun from above the front door with a dish cloth to avoid prints. I placed it under my mother's arm and carefully put her finger on the trigger. I then left quietly and sat on the front porch. I called 911 and reported a domestic violence incident.

The young deputy from the sheriff's office arrived in just a few minutes. When he got out of the car, I was still sitting on the front porch and pointed to the door. As I expected, he knocked loudly on the front door and yelled "Sheriff's department." The noise was loud enough to wake my mother and the shotgun went off, killing my father instantly. No charges were ever filed in this case. And no one had any suspicions that I had been involved other than calling 911.

Could I kill? Of course, I can kill. I killed my own father.

Chapter 10

Johnston

The name on my birth certificate is Clayton Delaney. Later, I became Chuck Johnston, and I retained very little of my previous life. Clayton Delaney could not survive in the world I live in now.

My early years were not remarkable in any way. I grew up just outside of Columbus, Ohio. My father owned a real estate agency in the suburbs of Columbus. Next door to his office was an insurance agency and he owned half of that as well. Year after year he made good money on both businesses. My mother, a trained accountant, kept the books at the Methodist Church we all attended every week. My parents were both very religious and the church was the center of their lives.

By the time I was six or seven I had decided that the Bible stories I heard at church had no more credibility than the Santa Claus or tooth fairy myths. Heaven and hell were abstractions that I could just not accept. The threat of going to hell forever if I was not good, whatever that means, was an empty threat. When my grandmother died, I was certain that I would never see her again and that she was not living the good life in heaven or enjoying the fires of hell. She was simply gone.

These anti-religious feelings were reinforced by our annual vacations. Once a year my parents would take a ten- or twelve-day vacation. Most of the time we would visit national parks or spend time on a lake or on some beach. When I was fourteen or so, we took our only trip to Europe. While this was only a brief introduction to the rest of the world, I did encounter Muslims and discovered that not everyone held the same religious beliefs. I then began to wonder about the different brands of religion and why some people were Methodists, others Catholic or Muslim. Much to my parents' surprise and horror, I refused to go back to church when we got home. Still, I am probably more of an agnostic than an evangelical atheist. I even questioned the Ten Commandments. Could I steal if I was hungry? Of course. Could I kill to defend myself or someone close to me? Absolutely.

My steadfast refusal to attend church caused a major rift between me and my parents. It also caused a rift between my parents. My mother continued to insist on my church attendance, while my father simply said: "Let the boy make up his own mind. He is going to do that anyway." Our happy little family was never quite the same. I felt that I had grown up and could make decisions of any kind for myself. Making up my own mind and making my own decisions proved to be very useful by the time I was in high school.

In high school I did some of the stupid things that teenagers often do. I discovered that I liked to drink alcoholic beverages of almost any variety. I discovered girls and had a more serious relationship than I should have had at that age. I was never arrested for doing stupid things, but I probably should have been. Despite these youthful follies, my grades were good and as a junior I qualified for a National Merit Scholarship.

I was not very athletic, but I was fast, faster than most of my friends. My father wanted me to try out for football or basketball hoping I could get an athletic scholarship to The Ohio State University. I knew better. I refused and instead tried out for the track team. I was good enough to come in second or third in some events and I was the fastest runner on the relay team. Still, I understood that I was not good enough to compete at the collegiate level. I still run three or four miles every day and I have done reasonably well in some half-marathons. Running is a useful talent in my current occupation, but it is just one of many skills necessary to work for the Agency.

My parents wanted me to attend nearby OSU, but by the time I was a senior in high school, they were no longer a meaningful part of my decision-making. My father, the respected businessman and ultra-religious member of the Methodist hurch, was arrested for insurance fraud early in my senior year. It seems that he had been filing false insurance claims on various rental properties which he owned through his real estate agency. Despite spending a small fortune on defense lawyers, he was convicted and sent off to prison for 18 months.

My mother died soon after he was sent to prison. The doctors said it was heart failure. More likely it was just embarrassment. Since I was only two weeks away from turning eighteen, child protective services allowed me to stay in the house and finish high school. I decided then that I should get far away from Columbus and that I should possibly shed the Delaney name. I had never liked my last name, mainly because of the popularity of Tom T. Hall's song "I remember the day that Clayton Delaney died."

I wanted no part of OSU, and I did not even apply. Instead, I sent applications to Stanford, Texas, and MIT. All three schools had excellent computer science programs and that was what I was looking for. Surprisingly, I was admitted to all three. I chose Stanford where I double majored in mathematics and computer science.

Stanford was a good place to be as an undergraduate. It was far from Ohio and none of my classmates knew about my criminal father. I soon became fascinated with networks including the mathematical theory of networks and the computational difficulties associated with networks.

This may seem like an obscure topic, but it is not. Networks are everywhere and they affect all parts of modern life. Everyone has heard of computer networks but that is not all. Transportation systems are networks. The human brain and nervous system are networks. There are social networks and even networks of spies. Oil and gas pipelines are also networks. Modern science is just beginning to understand networks and how fragile they can be. A disruption in one part of a network can lead to catastrophic failure in entire systems.

I tried to learn everything I could about networks. I took courses in several disciplines about networks. I was even allowed to take graduate courses in network theory and computation. I wrote my senior thesis on the spoke and hub networks often used by major airlines. I maintained that no one had ever demonstrated that the spoke and hub system was the most efficient way of organizing air traffic. The spoke and hub system might work for a small regional airline flying to a limited number of airports, but even this is difficult to demonstrate. Even this limited system depends on the reaction of competitors and the increased costs of congestion at the hub airport. For a large airline, there is clearly no analytical solution. The best that can be done is thousands of simulations and this approach does not tell the airline where to put its hub or how many hubs it should have to operate efficiently.

My plan was to pursue an advanced degree and continue my attempts to understand networks. My plan was put on hold when I was approached by Simulation Systems Computing, Inc (SSCI), a consulting firm specializing in analyzing oil and gas pipeline networks. SSCI had offices in Houston and Austin. They offered me more money than I had ever dreamed of making and told me I could locate in Austin and simultaneously undertake graduate work at UT. It was an offer I could not refuse.

In Austin, the work was fascinating, the city was great fun, and my graduate courses were as good as anything I took at Stanford. I used my knowledge of networks and computational algorithms to solve several interesting questions about pipelines and pipeline security. Where were the most vulnerable places on a pipeline? The answer is not as easy as it might seem. Sometimes the answers were counterintuitive. To identify where a vulnerability exists, you need to know a lot about pressure, volume, distance, the diameter of the pipes, the nodes of the network, and where the pipelines are above the surface. For one gas company, we found six previously unknown locations on the pipeline where well-placed explosives could do enough damage to bring operations to a halt. But the greatest vulnerability turned out to be the software that controlled the pipelines. A hacker could do more damage to the system than explosives by increasing pressure in one place and decreasing pressure in another. Worse still, it took me and a colleague only a couple of hours to access the company's computer system.

I had been at SSCI for about a year when we got a contract with London Energy Consultants (LEC). Yes, this was the same firm that had offices in the BDSM building that Ross had visited. I had met Ross in Austin and it was fortunate that he did not recognize me when I interviewed him in Vienna. Ten years, a different name and completely different context saved the day.

The contract with LEC was to evaluate the capacity of the EU to use more natural gas from Russia. Nordstream 1 was already in operation and Russia's natural gas exporting firm, Gazprom, wanted to sell even more to Europe. Building Nordstream 2 would make the EU more dependent on Russia. Gazprom contracted with LEC which quickly learned that it did not have the expertise to do the job. SSCI had the expertise and agreed to the sub-contract. This contract took me to

Europe where I toured natural gas facilities in several nations. Like Darwin on his various voyages, I learned a lot from simple observation. I also met and became friends with several Gazprom executives and engineers. I maintained these relationships and stay in close touch with them even now.

The work at SSCI was good fun and I made lots of money. I could see myself working for them for a long time and retiring at a very early age. Sadly, the management at SSCI was not as competent as the technical staff. SSCI bid on and was awarded several contracts that proved to be huge money losers. The firm was soon in serious financial trouble, and I was looking for work. Among other places, I applied to the Agency and after several months I was hired at a much lower salary than I had been accustomed to at SSCI. No problem, I had banked a lot of my salary, and the prospect of a change of pace was attractive.

When I reported for work, really training, at Langley I was ushered into the Director's office before I had even met any of my fellow trainees. I was informed that I had been selected for an assignment after my training that required me to use a different name. Even at the Agency I was to be known as Chuck Johnston, no middle name. That was okay with me. Only two people at the Agency knew me as Clayton Delaney. That name was removed from all documentation. I had become Chuck Johnston. After several weeks of training, I was given a few days off. I took the time off to go to Ohio and change my name legally to Chuck Johnston. By this time, my father had been released from prison, but I did not bother to go see him. I was no longer Clayton Delaney.

I returned to Langley and was given my first assignment. Along with another agent, I was told to keep tabs on Abdul Mohammed Zaire, a member or perhaps former member, of Hezbollah. Abdul had been traveling in Europe ostensibly to purchase natural gas pipeline equipment

112

and the software to run it for Lebanon. Abdul was also suspected of running a terrorist group, responsible for several deaths and many more injuries. My expertise in natural gas pipelines should allow me to meet and interact with him. I did connect with him at a gas pipeline equipment show in Brussels. We had drinks after the second day of the show, and it soon became apparent that he had little expertise in natural gas pipelines or the industry in general. I also discovered that he had a mistress in a flat not far away from the show and that he returned to Brussels frequently. Without much difficulty, I identified two others who were watching Abdul. I had met one of the followers, a jovial fellow from MI6. The other one I did not know, but I was confident that he was a professional.

Abdul traveled a lot. From Brussels, he went to Budapest, Athens, and Istanbul. I followed. Everywhere Abdul traveled, someone was killed. Sometimes more than one. In Budapest, the unfortunate victim was the Economic Attaché in the US Embassy. In Athens, it was the cultural affairs officer in the British Embassy. In Istanbul it was my colleague in the Agency, a well-respected and experienced agent, and his wife. All had been shot in the back of the head at close range. In Istanbul, I was not far away from the shootings which took place near Taksim Square. While I did not see the shootings, I did see Abdul walking casually away from the scene.

It was in Istanbul that I decided that Abdul must be eliminated. The myth is that the Agency does not officially sanction assassinations, but the Agency does not hesitate to identify the location of known terrorists for some other organization. After all, it was Agency personnel who identified the courier that led to Bin Laden in Pakistan. It was the Agency that established the location of Al Baghdadi, the ISIS leader, and many others. Sometimes, bad people just end up dead. In these cases, the

Agency never takes credit, but there is often little doubt about who did it.

The Agency never trains its agents to be killers. There is no need. They are taught self-defense skills and all agents must become proficient in the use of a variety of firearms. Agents are also taught how to identify potential threats and the imaginative ways that an attacker might try to kill them. No need to practice killing. By the time we were finished training, we all knew how to avoid being killed and, always unspoken, we knew how to kill.

Killing Abdul was not an option. It was a moral imperative. Abdul was a thoroughly evil person who was responsible for killing many. There was no doubt he would kill many more. There was also no question about how to do it, once I had decided not to bring in my friend from MI6. No one should know about it but me. Naturally I wanted Abdul to understand who had done it.

I chose the golf course. Abdul loved to play golf, but he was not very good at it. On the seventh hole, he almost always sliced his shot with the ball ending up in the woods near the fairway. On that Tuesday morning I was waiting for him in the woods. As expected, Abdul entered the woods and after some looking, bent down to pick up the ball. I was fifteen feet away and softly said "Abdul." When he looked up, I put a single round in his forehead, killing him instantly. No one was likely to hear the shot because the woods were adjacent to a major highway. I left quickly, jumped on my rented motorbike, and sped down the highway – confident that no one had seen me.

I never intended to become a killer, but I knew that this first killing was not likely to be my last.

Chapter 11
The Mystery Woman

Johnston and Hinton called me the mystery woman. They claimed that I showed up in unexpected places and that no amount of effort could identify me or figure out what I was doing. The Agency had used facial recognition software and found nothing. Inquiries with Interpol and other international agencies came up with no information about me. Was I a killer? If so, who was paying for my services? Was I old or young? They simply did not know and that was a very good thing for me.

My father was in the German diplomatic corps. He met my Pakistani mother in his early twenties on his first overseas assignment. Their relationship was tumultuous from the beginning. My mother's parents were wealthy, upper-class Pakistanis with political ambitions. They had made their money in real estate in Karachi. In truth, they were slumlords of a sort. They had inherited a lot of land in Karachi, built small houses and apartments and rented them at exorbitant rates. Karachi had been a relatively small port city before partition but grew rapidly after that and it continues to grow today. In many respects, Karachi was not a pleasant place to live. They moved to Lahore and later to the new capital of Islamabad. They traveled frequently, mainly to Europe and occasionally to resorts in Mexico and the Caribbean. Nominally, they were Muslims, but their true religion was money. They eventually sold most of their properties in Karachi, but they continued to make money in foreign exchange markets, usually by shorting the Pakistani Rupee.

My grandparents were outraged when my dad began showing romantic interest in my mother. No, they did not care about his total lack of religion. They did not care that he was German. They were sophisticated internationalists. The problem was that my dad did not have a lot of money. He was just a junior member of the diplomatic corps. Their assessment was that his future career was limited. They had loftier goals for their only child. They were active politically and hoped that one day their daughter, my mother, would become prime minister of Pakistan. If Benazir Bhutto could do it, why not their child. They did not want to handicap her with an ill-chosen husband. They made it as difficult as possible for the young lovers and let them both know that marriage was out of the question.

Apparently, the tension between my grandparents and parents did not stop when my mother became pregnant with me. For upper-class Pakistanis, an out-of-wedlock pregnancy is more of a problem than it would have been in Europe or elsewhere in the west. It is socially disgraceful and would end any political ambitions. In any case my grandparents held a hurried traditional wedding for my parents but did not speak to them for years after that allegedly happy event.

The tension between my parents and grandparents eventually caused marital problems with my parents. On more than one occasion they lived apart but after months, in one case after two years, they got back together. Meanwhile, my father's career progressed nicely, and he was assigned to some much sought-after locations – Hong Kong, Paris, Rome, and Washington, DC. I got to live in all these places and more.

My parents insisted that I had the best education possible. When it came time for a university, I chose the Sorbonne. I excelled at languages since I was already fluent in French, English, German, and Urdu but my passion was for acting. I learned that I could play almost any part from

116

comedy to serious drama. I took classes in make-up and could transform myself into almost any character. Once, I even got to play Romeo in Shakespeare's play. It was not so difficult to dress as a man or to perform a male role. I was rather flat-chested at the time, and I had taken enough voice classes to pass as a young male adult.

There were two non-academic events that shaped my life at the Sorbonne. One night after leaving the theater a little later than usual, a man I had never seen before attempted to rape me. He was almost successful, but my martial arts skills ultimately came to my rescue. I left him in considerable pain in the alley he had dragged me into. Most men are so stupid that they don't think a woman can defend themselves. Still, the incident frightened me and taught me to be very cautious and alert to danger at all times. I promised myself to do even more damage if I ever encountered this man or anyone like him again.

I did not report the incident to the police or to the authorities at the Sorbonne. Why bother? The police would have little evidence to go on. No rape took place. There would be no DNA evidence or any evidence for that matter. It would just be my word against his even though I knew that I could identify him.

For a few weeks, my life seemed to return to normal. I suspected that the man who had attacked me was a graduate student, but there was no sign of him on campus and I did not see him elsewhere. I had quickly returned to my usual daily habits, which included an early morning jog/run in the beautiful Jardin du Luxembourg adjacent to the Sorbonne. My runs were always followed by a coffee and a croissant from one of the nearby groceries or cafes. It was the most relaxing time of the day.

I had little fear of a daylight attack and I felt increasingly confident and relaxed until one Tuesday morning while on my run, he stepped out from behind some bushes, facing me. He had a knife, and he made no attempt to conceal his face. "This time I am ready for you," he said. As he approached, I said "Not again. I am getting tired of this." Without any hesitation I knew exactly what to do. I faked a kick to his crotch and instinctively he brought his hands down to protect himself. It was no contest. I turned the knife in his direction and with his own hand pushed it as far as I could into his intestines. He stood there in shock for a couple of seconds and this time my kick to his crotch was viciously on target. He collapsed and I ran as fast as I could toward the exit, leaving him bleeding and in pain on the path.

I had no regrets, and I did not learn that he had died until two days later from a small article in the paper. Again, I did not bother to report anything to the police. I had no doubt that the police might look for a suspect and perhaps they did but no one ever came to question me. After a few days of being terrified that I was about to be arrested for murder, I began to relax and even resumed my morning runs in a different area of the park. This was the first time I killed anyone. It was not my last.

The other life-changing event that occurred while I was at the Sorbonne was that I met the only man I ever truly loved. Yes, it is true that I had several lovers, both men and women, but I never really loved any of them. They were just for amusement and experimentation with my undefined sexuality. Rabbani, the same man that Hinton and others nicknamed The Rabbi, was different. He was also the most reluctant lover I ever met. Most of my lovers were eager to hop into bed with me. Rabbani was not.

We met accidentally at a café where I often purchased my coffee and croissant after a morning run. He too liked a morning coffee and croissant before he went to class at the Sorbonne. The first few times I noticed him at the café, we ignored each other. I had no interest in him at all. Still, I found myself going to that café more often than usual.

Eventually, I sat down at his table and introduced myself, explaining that since we were regulars at the café, we should at least know each other by name. Rabbani was, at least then, a shy man who seemed almost embarrassed that I had approached him. At that first meeting, we exchanged names but not phone numbers. I told him that I looked forward to seeing him at the café again sometime.

Shy or not, Rabbani was at the café two days later and I again sat down at his table. I did not ask if he had been there the day before, but he later admitted that he had been. This time, the small talk was a little easier, but not much easier. I learned that he was a Saudi. He learned a little about my multi-national background. For the first time, he did smile as I got up to leave and said he hoped to see me again at the café. Again, we parted without exchanging phone numbers, email addresses, or any other way to get in touch.

I had not previously thought of him as a potential lover. I was naturally friendly and out-going. I had only thought of him as a potential friend. I had many casual friends, some of them good friends, without ever considering them as objects of sexual desire. I went somewhere else for coffee the next day and the day after that. Then I started to miss him, and I knew that I wanted to make him my new lover. That should have been simple enough. No one had resisted me before. It was not simple, and it was painfully slow. It took me four weeks of coffee and croissants before he finally suggested dinner. The rest was easier. After dinner and a couple of glasses of wine, we returned to my very small apartment on Rue Madame.

For the rest of the academic year, we were rarely apart. Soon after that first night, Rabbani stayed at my small apartment almost every night. We shared everything including intimate details of our lives. I felt comfortable enough with him to tell him about killing my would-be attacker. I jokingly told him that for the right amount of money, I could become a paid assassin. He laughed and told me of an event he had been involved in in his home village. We were happy. I think he loved me as much as I loved him, but it did not last.

At the end of the academic year, he told me that he just had to learn more about the economics of the oil industry. His future depended on it. He was going to finish his degree at the London School of Economics. Later he would go to graduate school at the University of Texas. We tried to keep the relationship going while he was in London. He visited me a couple of times in Paris, and I sometimes went to London. Both of us knew that it could not work that way and we reluctantly agreed to put our relationship on hold.

We have kept in touch ever since even though Rabbani married Shabazz. Who could blame him? She was and is gorgeous and smart. Then, one day I got a call from Rabbani. He wanted to meet. We met secretly on a trail just outside of Grindelwald, Switzerland. I anticipated a renewal of our relationship. I should have known better. He wanted to take me up on my offer to become a paid assassin. I was stunned but I readily agreed. I would have done anything for him and still would.

Rabbani paid me a million Euros to kill an ex-pat Saudi who had become a real threat to the dominance of the oil industry. As part of the agreement, I was given a Saudi passport under the name of Sheila Khalid. For the passport photo, I used my best acting makeup skills and looked like a very different person—a forty-five-year-old woman. Even my facial bone structure looked different. The most difficult part was my eyes, but I managed to obtain contact lenses that were a different color and had a different pattern in the iris. No facial recognition was possible. I now had three passports. One from the EU, one from Pakistan, and one was the Saudi passport. All three passports had photos of me in various disguises. Only the Pakistani passport had my real name.

Killing the Saudi ex-pat was easier than I thought it would be. No trip to the Kingdom was needed. The intended victim resided in Brussels, a city I knew well. I would have preferred to use a knife but my Glock with a silencer was a better choice because it was hard to get close enough for the knife. I shot him as he was entering his apartment one night after a late dinner. I knew I had killed him with one shot to the head. I was the only one on the street and made an easy exit by entering his building. As promised, a million Euros was deposited in an account in a bank in Geneva under the name Sheila Khalid. I was set financially for life and thought that was the end of my career as an assassin.

Three months later, Rabbani called and told me to buy another cell phone and activate it under some false name. He told me to text him the number and that I would receive a call from a friend. I could do what I wanted when the friend called. It was nearly a week before the new cell phone rang. My target this time was an oil industry executive who had been working with Boko Haram to disrupt Nigerian oil production in a misguided and futile effort to increase world oil prices. I told the caller that I would need a million Euros deposited in Sheila Khalid's account in the Geneva bank before carrying out this job and another million Euros after the job had been completed. The caller simply said it was worth every penny. After checking out the caller's story, I did the job efficiently and quietly.

My next job had nothing to do with the oil industry other than the fact that the caller turned out to be an oil industry executive. I was told that the client's wife was a nasty and mean woman who had also been sleeping with at least three other men. I told the caller my terms and checked out his story. I had never killed another woman, but I was only momentarily put off by that fact. I did that job and some others. I was never in danger of being caught.

I am still for hire if you have enough money. My current lover is Cindy Burgess.

Chapter 12

The Rabbi

I was born in Al-Bakr, a small village in Saudi Arabia not far from the border with Yemen. In many respects, the village was more progressive than you would expect in such a remote part of the world. The village had running water and a sewage system long before any other place within hundreds of miles. Nearly a century ago, the village brought in electricity – again, far sooner than any other village within many miles. Houses were well-built and the school was a source of pride for nearly everyone in the community.

The village also had a long-standing legacy of religious tolerance as well as a tolerance for ideas from outside. Early in its history, the village was over-run by a group of Jews. The villagers were told that they must convert to Judaism and abandon their Pagan Gods on penalty of death. Nearly everyone in the village converted to Judaism. The Jewish era lasted more than a century until an even more aggressive band of Christians descended on the village and told the villagers that they must convert to Christianity – again on penalty of death if they refused. The Christian era in Al-Bakr lasted nearly three centuries before the Muslims arrived and once again informed the villagers that they must convert. Infidels would be executed. The villagers had been through this before and easily abandoned Christianity for Allah. This history is still alive and well in Al-Bakr, passed down from one generation to the next along with a pronounced skepticism for absolutes and a willingness to adapt to changing circumstances. Religious and ideological tolerance is a major part of who I am.

The village, however, had no tolerance of thieves, adulterers, child abusers, and other miscreants. There was no formal police department in Al-Bakr. When a crime was committed, the village elders would meet, seek to obtain the facts of the case, and impose punishment if necessary. Punishment was harsh and there was no appeal to some higher court. Drinking alcohol was punished with the whip as it is in much of the Kingdom today. More serious crimes could be punished more severely – including execution. Everyone growing up in Al-Bakr was aware of the harsh treatment of those who had done wrong. No one, including me, thought it was wrong to severely punish, even kill, very bad people. This is something worth understanding about me. Harsh punishment for wrongdoers is justified, whether the punishment is carried out by a legal system, consensus of elders, or an individual. You must understand this attitude if you are to understand who I am.

Another part of village life was a remarkable educational system. All children, including girls, were required to attend school from the ages of six to sixteen. A curious child could learn languages (Arabic, French, and English), history, literature, mathematics, and be exposed to basic scientific principles. The local school system was probably as good as what can be found in other places. School taught me that there was a larger world than could be found in the confines of the village limits. A few lucky students, including me, went on to colleges and universities while the rest were well-prepared for life in the village. An appreciation of the value of education is also a part of me.

Intense loyalty was also part of village life. Residents of Al-Bakr seemed to have loyalty as an inherited trait. Loyalty to family and friends was unquestioned. If a family member or close friend needed help, it was freely given. No questions asked. What is a little unusual is that the residents were, almost without exception, extremely loyal to the village itself. Indeed, they were more loyal to the village than to Allah or any other god that they might have worshipped. The village had a higher priority than some distant national government and the royal family. I learned at an early age that loyalty was a virtue that makes decision-making in difficult circumstances almost automatic. You simply don't abandon a friend in need.

Village life was good, but I wanted and needed more education than could be offered there. My school record was a good one and I had always excelled on standardized tests. My record allowed me to enroll in King Abdullah University of Science and Technology (KAUST) in Thuwal. KAUST had a lot to offer. Thuwal is on the Red Sea and it is a gorgeous place to study. In truth there is not much in Thuwal except KAUST but that did not matter. I did not know it at the time, but KAUST would soon be ranked among the best 100 universities in the world. Students and faculty came from dozens of countries because of its reputation. No expense had been spared in constructing the campus or its surroundings. Ali Al-Naimi, the former Saudi oil minister, chaired the committee to design the campus and the curriculum. It was the first mixed gender university in Saudi Arabia and the religious police do not operate there.

I learned a lot at KAUST, especially the value of basic research in nearly all areas. I thoroughly enjoyed the area and for the first time interacting with women on a more or less equal basis. For the first time, I learned that women were smart, hard-working and determined. My time at KAUST would end sooner than I expected. Two faculty members called me aside one day and they both had the same advice for me. They told me I could get an excellent education without leaving KAUST, but they had noted a curiosity in me about the rest of the world that could not be satisfied there. They advised me to enroll in an older, more established university in another country. When I asked them which university, both replied that the Sorbonne was probably the best place to go. They told me it was a great university in a great cosmopolitan city, and it was 800 years old while KAUST was brand new. I should go there, they said, while I was young enough to be open to new ideas and experiences.

I applied to Sorbonne and was soon on my way to a new adventure. I loved Paris, enjoyed my classes, but in all honesty many of the classes were not as good as the ones at KAUST. It was at a café near the Sorbonne that I met the woman that Hinton and Johnston call the mystery woman. Let them wonder who she is. I will not tell them or anyone else. Loyalty is truly important.

To this day I am not certain what her real name is, but I will call her Sheila Khalid. Soon after that chance encounter, we were in love and for all practical purposes I moved in with her. Sheila changed my life. She taught me about sex for the sake of enjoyment. We laughed a lot. Later she taught me about heartbreak.

If we had thought about it, we would have known from the beginning that our relationship as lovers would not last forever. I am to blame for an early ending to our affair. In less than a year at the Sorbonne I had discovered that my intellectual passion was to learn about the economics of the oil and gas industry. The Sorbonne was the wrong place to do that. Economics at Sorbonne was too constrained by tradition—both the ancient tradition of the French physiocrats as well as a strong Marxist tendency among the faculty. I had decided to transfer to the London School of Economics (LSE) to finish my degree. We tried to carry on a long-distance relationship for a while with me in London and

Sheila in Paris. It did not work the way we wanted it to work. Long distance romances are just very difficult.

When we decided to quit pretending and end it, Sheila jokingly said to keep in touch and that if I ever needed her services as an assassin to let her know. Earlier she had told me about killing her potential attacker in the park. I was almost certain that she was joking. We did keep in touch, and we will always be in touch. She is a soulmate. She is an important part of my life despite the fact that we are no longer lovers. Little did I know that I would take her up on this offer soon after I became the chief economist at the Saudi Ministry of Energy.

I finished my degree at LSE with honors in economics. I still wanted to know more about the economics of oil. The logical place to pursue my studies was the University of Texas at Austin. UT had a long tradition of analyzing the oil industry. The faculty there also had a strong sense of history. They understood that the industry did not just suddenly appear as a variable in some arcane mathematical model. That is where I wanted to go and I did.

Austin is a wonderful place, perhaps best described by the city's motto: Keep Austin Weird. The Economics Department was also just what I needed. The department had an eclectic group of faculty and a tightly knit cohort of graduate students. Shortly after I arrived in Austin, I met Eddie Hinton who quickly nicknamed me The Rabbi. I offered mild protests at this nickname, but it made me smile internally. I liked it and more importantly, I knew that I had been accepted as part of the graduate student gang.

Hinton and I became very good friends and remain so today. In many respects I regard him as the brother I never had. We studied together. We ate together. We even pursued the same woman, my wife Shabazz, for a while. Hinton was disappointed but not angry when it

127

became clear that Shabazz had chosen me over him. He soon met Linda whom he later married. Hinton introduced me to Mexican food, draft beer at Scholz's Garden, two swimming pools (Barton Springs and Hippie Hollow), as well as Austin's music on sixth street. Others pretended to know about the oil and gas industry without really understanding it. Hinton's knowledge of it was genuine. He never faked anything.

Now, whenever Hinton wants to contact me, he sends a text with this message: "Rabbi, where the hell are you? You owe me a dinner." Whenever I want to contact him, I send the same message but substitute "Professor" for Rabbi. Neither one of us are after a free meal. I trust Hinton more than anyone else except perhaps Shabazz. I would do almost anything for my friend.

Ross was in the same graduate school cohort as Hinton and me. I knew him but we were never close. Ross always seemed to be a bit standoffish or shy. He was a marginal member of the graduate school gang. My only contact with him now is to provide credentials for him at OPEC meetings. I don't mind doing that and he seems to appreciate it a lot. I do not invite him to dinner, and I do not accept his invitations.

Johnston, the CIA guy that Hinton introduced me to, is looking for a killer and intrigue in the oil industry. I don't trust him. I won't help him. I could almost laugh at him. I would surely be on his suspect list if he knew that I was in DC when Patti Walker was killed and in London when Annie Stoddard was killed. And, of course, I know the mystery woman.

PART 3

Another Time, Another Place

Chapter 13

Backtracking

Shortly after noon the next day, Hinton called Millie, the fixer.

"Hi Millie, I hope I have not caused you too much trouble but how are the IT guys doing on my problem?"

"The IT experts are amazing. With little information to work with, they have taken down your alleged social media accounts and the blog. Even more amazing is that they found the guilty party, the man who did this to you. His name is Rasheed al-Salmon, and he apparently works in the Saudi Ministry of Energy where your friend the Rabbi works."

"Millie, I love you, but I am going to hang up and call the Rabbi. Thank you more than you will ever know."

Excited and anxious, Hinton called the Rabbi.

"Rabbi, I have news for you. Millie and the IT experts at OU have taken down the fake social media posts and the blog. They also found out who made these posts. His name is Rasheed al-Salmon and he works in your office."

"I am very familiar with him. He is a disgruntled employee who thought he should be promoted. I did not promote him, and he is probably trying to embarrass me by causing trouble for you. I will take care of this, but it will be delicate. He is the second cousin of the Crown Prince. It will take me a day or two, but I have friends who can help. I can't fire him because of his connections to the Crown Prince. Rasheed will be given his promotion and an important title. I think he will become the chief-of-staff to our Ambassador to Chad. If that doesn't work, he might become the public relations officer for the Waste Management Division of the City of Riyadh. In either case, he will no longer be a problem. In a few months, you can probably return to the Kingdom, and we will make certain that you get to visit the Line."

"Thank you, my friend. I look forward to seeing you again soon. I'll let you go for now so that you can attend to Rasheed."

Hinton decided to take the train from Vienna to Paris and then take the Eurostar to London. He could use the ticket he had purchased to the airport another time or throw it away. The Paris train would not depart until 9 pm. Hinton had time on his hands. He checked his bags at the will-call booth in the station and walked around Vienna taking in the sights. Later he returned to the station and sent a text to Johnston telling him of his travel itinerary. He bought a newspaper, the last John le Carre novel, and had a late lunch in the station. He still had time on his hands and although he looked forward to his time on the train to think about what he had been doing and what he might do next, the Vienna train station was not the place to do it.

He walked outside and called Linda. Hinton was not oblivious to the time differences between Vienna and Oklahoma City, but he knew that Linda was probably awake and had the coffee pot brewing already. She liked expensive blends. Linda had other expensive habits as well, but Hinton had never objected or even thought much about it while they were married. After all, she consistently made more money than he did.

When Linda answered the phone by saying "You must be bored." Hinton smiled and said, "I am not bored. I just want to hear your voice." He could tell from her voice that she was not the least bit angry and that she was awake and probably finishing her first cup of coffee. This turned out to be true. Fortunately, she was also alone. They talked for a long time. As the conversation went on, Hinton realized that it was the first open and honest conversation they had had in many years. They talked about everything.

Hinton explained where he was and generally what he was doing. He left out some of the details, especially any hint that there was danger involved in his current endeavors. Linda knew him well and was not fooled into thinking he had divulged everything he knew. Eventually, he admitted to everything. He told her about Ross, the Agency guy Johnston, his trip to DC, London, and his brief stop in Paris, and even the mystery woman. For some reason he did not talk about his trip to Riyadh. Hinton was not worried about someone listening in on the phone call. Very sophisticated software would be required to decipher the encryption on his phone. To an outsider the phone call would look like it had come from someone else.

Eventually, the conversation turned more personal. Linda mentioned that when she asked for a divorce that she was not really after a divorce. What she had wanted was for Hinton to declare his undying love and confess to how much he needed her. For his part, Hinton said he did not want a divorce either but that he thought that their marriage could not last if she wanted out of it. There was no point in trying to get her to stay if she did not want to. Both lamented the fact that neither one of them had been honest about what they needed. Linda said that they had both moved on and that there was no use in trying to pretend otherwise. Some things are just not reversible. They were both proud of their daughter, Leslie, who was doing well in San Diego, but they greatly regretted the fact that their divorce had been so hard on her. So much for adults knowing what was right. They laughed.

Linda offered unsolicited advice about Millie. "Don't try to change your relationship with Millie. We had lunch last week and she said you were making noises about doing so. Don't even think about it. She is not going to sleep with you. She will not marry you. The only thing you can get out of trying to change your relationship is trouble or a broken heart. She can be your best friend, even your BFF, but she doesn't want more."

Linda had never given him advice on how to conduct his life – even when they were married. He wondered if this was coming from Millie or if Linda had a not so hidden agenda. He told Linda of his concerns. Linda said she had no hidden agenda. She was not telling him this to keep the door open to their relationship. She said this was what she had gathered from Millie, who had not asked her to tell him this. Millie could speak for herself as she always had.

Their conversation turned to more mundane things. Linda asked about Fergie and said she was glad that he had such a loyal companion. They talked about Big Bend. They talked about the pleasures and nuisances of owning a home. They talked about their careers and about the sorry state of contemporary country music. Neither one of them liked the blend of country and rock that so often passed for country. The old country singers had lived the hard times and lost loves they were singing about.

Hinton felt good about their conversation and thought it could have gone on much longer, but it was already close to departure time for the train. Hinton would have a lot to think about on a long train ride and now he was in the mood to do that. He reminded himself to be analytical and honest with himself about what he wanted and what was going on with his Agency mission. So he boarded the train, sat in his assigned window seat and was relieved that there were only a few passengers in his car. He could ponder the universe all he liked without interruption. He looked forward to the long ride.

As the train pulled out of the Vienna station, Hinton was relaxed and looking forward to the journey. He had several things to sort out and decided to take care of the easiest thing first. This was a habit he had acquired as an undergraduate. If you have a lot of things on your to do list, get one of them done. Always choose the easiest one and finish it. That will give you a sense of accomplishment and give you some hope that the rest of the list can be finished as well. It was a way of avoiding despair and panic.

The easiest thing on his list was to prepare a lecture that he had agreed to give at the London School of Economics. He wanted this lecture to be a good one that might impress the Nigerian student Rose that OU was the place to go for her doctorate. He knew that he could walk into a room and give a lecture on the history of the oil industry and many other topics without preparation. He had done so successfully many times, but this was a special occasion and at least some advance thought was essential. Besides, going over some of this history might help him understand what was happening now with the transition and the promise of market disruption.

Hinton had any number of topics he could have chosen. Technological change was one of his favorites. The industry had been developing new techniques and new equipment since its beginning. It was a remarkable story, but Hinton rejected it, in part, because audiences tended to get bored with technical details. Security and other vulnerabilities were among his favorites. He understood all too well how natural disasters, terrorists, and simple stupidity could bring enough of the industry to a halt and impose chaos on economies world-wide. Hinton rejected this topic as well. Guilt was the problem. Someone in the audience might pick up some new knowledge on how to make a mess of the industry.

Hinton decided to speak about deception, fraud, and illegal activities which have always been a major part of the industry and remain so today. These were good stories involving fascinating characters who shaped one of the world's most important industries. He would need to be careful not to leave the impression that everyone in the industry was dishonest and had evil intentions. That was not the case. He had grown to admire the hard-working, dedicated people who delivered products that most people don't ever think about. Yes, that was a good choice. Audiences always loved these tales.

His lecture should begin at the beginning. That was easy. The industry began with fraud or at least deception. Colonel Edwin L. Drake is credited with drilling the first commercial oil well in the US in 1859. Colonel Drake was not a Colonel and there is no record of him ever serving in the military. Drake had been a conductor on a railroad and that was the only uniform he ever wore. He acquired the title by having his friends write him letters delivered to the local post-office addressed to Colonel Drake. This was not an unusual practice at the time. Drake was hardly a wildcatter. He drilled his well on the banks of Oil Creek, where oil seeped naturally from the ground. His well was less than 70 feet deep.

Later, it was often falsely said that Drake's well was the first in the world. It was not. Two years earlier an oil well had been drilled in La Brea, Trinidad. About the same time, wells were drilled in West Virginia, Poland, and elsewhere. Long before that, the Chinese had drilled wells in the fourth century A.D. The Drake well origin myth is a suitable story for an industry filled with falsehoods and chicanery.

Next, he would talk about the Standard Oil case. Barely a decade after Drake drilled his well, John D. Rockefeller had acquired a near monopoly on oil in Ohio and soon expanded his holdings in other parts of the US. What Rockefeller accomplished was market share and vertical integration. He eventually had a near monopoly on exploration and drilling, refining, transportation, and marketing. That combination can't be beat if your goal is to maximize profit.

But in 1890, Congress passed the Sherman Antitrust Act. The Sherman Act is a beautiful piece of legislation, and it is only a couple of pages long. Can you imagine how long it might be if it were enacted today? After Congressional staffers and lawyers got through with it, the act would be hundreds of pages of arcane, almost impossible to read, legislation. The short story is that the Sherman Act declared any trust, combination, or conspiracy in restraint of trade to be illegal. In 1911, the Supreme Court declared Standard Oil of New Jersey, Rockefeller's company, to be in violation of the Sherman Act and broke up the firm into more than 30 different firms. Never mind that over the decades to come, many of these companies would be consolidated again. Rockefeller and Standard Oil would always be regarded by the public as criminals.

Then, Hinton decided he would talk about the granddaddy of all scandals, Teapot Dome. In the early 1920s, Secretary of the Interior Albert B. Fall, in exchange for bribes, leased federal land in Wyoming (Teapot Dome) and California to oil companies at very low rates and without a bidding process. Fall was exposed by a Senate investigation and ultimately, he became the first cabinet secretary to go to prison. The scandal nearly ended the presidency of Warren G. Harding, who had the good fortune to die before being indicted.

Hinton thought about telling the remarkable story of the Enron scandal which resulted in the downfall of several executives including prison time for some and the collapse of one of the largest accounting firms in the US—Arthur Andersen. The fact that Enron is still alive in the form of one of its spin-off companies, EOG Resources, always made him smile. But the Enron story was far too complicated for the time he had in this lecture. That story involved numerous subsidiaries, the transfer of bad assets to those subsidiaries, as well as some tricky accounting.

He also rejected the idea of talking about the depletion tax allowance, a mechanism that gave oil companies billions of dollars that most corporations would need to pay. The depletion allowance was not illegal, but it was facilitated by millions of dollars in bribes (oops, campaign donations) to members of Congress for decades. Imagine if GM or Ford could take a tax deduction on automobiles not yet produced because someday, they might not be able to produce them.

Instead, Hinton decided to tell the story of Chesapeake Energy, its sudden rise and equally rapid collapse. Chesapeake Energy was founded by Aubrey McClendon and his partner Tom Ward in 1989. Their total investment was $50,000. At its peak in the early 2000s, Chesapeake was worth many billions. Chesapeake started buying oil and gas leases in northwestern Oklahoma. They were mainly interested in gas production. The company soon expanded to the Barnett shale region in north Texas and later tried to extend their holdings to the Austin Chalk formation in east Texas.

Chesapeake was so successful that it became a favored stock on Wall Street. Chesapeake signed a deal to name the arena where the Oklahoma City Thunder would play NBA games. They built a huge campus for the company in Oklahoma City and hired thousands of employees. On his own, McClendon opened Pops 66, a very popular destination for Oklahomans and tourists. Pops was a combination gas station, convenience store, and seller of almost any variety of soda pop. Pops is still open in Arcadia, Oklahoma. Chesapeake was a big deal.

For many years, McClendon was known for paying too much for land leases but the need for profits drove him into some rather nefarious activities. In the early 2000s, there were rumors that he was not paying royalties due to lessees. There were also rumors that he was conspiring with other companies to rig prices on leases and that he was booking profits that did not exist to keep the share prices high. McClendon was ousted from the company when it became clear that he was using Chesapeake funds to finance his own private deals.

His activities were soon the subject of a US Department of Justice investigation. On May 1, 2016 McClendon was indicted on criminal charges for violating the antitrust laws. The indictment was based on his often successful attempts to collude with other companies to rig the price of leased land. McClendon was killed in a one car crash the next day. His car hit a bridge embankment at a very high speed. He may have been traveling at 90 miles per hour. He may have committed suicide, but no one knows for sure. Like Ken Lay, the former CEO of Enron, he avoided prison time by dying.

Hinton knew that he could go on for hours talking about various desperados in the oil and gas industry. He also knew that time was limited and that he should find a way to end his lecture. He did not want to leave the impression that everyone in the industry was a scoundrel. For each of the industry bad boys, he could name an equally famous and honest industry leader. He settled on George P. Mitchell.

Mitchell was a Texas oil and gas man and he remains a legend in the industry. In 1974 he founded The Woodlands, a gorgeous planned community near Houston which is now home to more than 100,000 people along with golf courses, conference centers, and company headquarters. The Woodlands, however, was not the source of his enduring legacy.

In the late 1970s, Mitchell's gas wells in north Texas were drying up. Mitchell, a geologist by training, was convinced that there were still vast quantities of natural gas locked in 250 feet of shale. In 1981, he began a quest that would take more than 15 years to unlock that gas from the shale rock. He started fracking and horizontal drilling. These were not new techniques. Fracking had begun during the Civil War when the Army started shooting artillery shells into wells to make oil flow easier. Horizontal drilling began in the late 1940s in Oklahoma allowing drillers to tap into oil on someone else's land. Mitchell combined the two techniques and became falsely known as the father of fracking. For years, he was unsuccessful, and he spent millions of dollars drilling unproductive wells. In 1997 he finally found a combination of water, sand, and chemicals that worked. Bingo, his depleted gas fields began producing large quantities and he became a legend.

Hinton picked Mitchell because his success also meant that Aubrey McClendon's leases were worth far more than anyone had ever guessed. They were not in business together. McClendon simply benefitted from the new techniques.

Hinton was pleased with himself for finishing what he knew would be a well-received lecture. The slow rocking of the train, the sounds, and smells of train travel, as well as the scenery added to his feeling of well-being. His second glass of a very good Beaujolais no doubt contributed to his good mood. He liked what he was doing. He was glad he had taken the train but knew that it was time to move on to a new topic.

Hinton was unsure of whether his love life or the murders and intrigue associated with the industry would be more difficult to handle. In his mind, he flipped a coin and decided to give his love life priority even though it was highly unlikely that he could solve that problem on a train. Perhaps he would never solve it.

Hinton was certain of one thing. He wanted a woman in his life, a permanent relationship if that were possible. He had thoroughly enjoyed his marriage to Linda, at least most of it until they had grown apart. That happened when their daughter Leslie was old enough that she had her own life to live and did not need the constant attention of one or both parents. She was a good kid, well behaved, with several good friends, active in school activities and an honor student. Except as occasional cheerleaders, her parents were no longer needed. He was more than pleased that even after the divorce there was no acrimony between them.

Hinton had adapted reasonably well to the single life. He was busy with work, and he enjoyed it. His career was on a fast track to anywhere he wanted it to go. He turned down attractive job offers on a regular basis. He could literally go anywhere he wanted. His daughter was a source of pride and she frequently consulted him long-distance on subjects that many young adults would not discuss with their parents. Fergie provided him with unconditional love and companionship. He also liked the fact that he and Linda had lunch or dinner together on a regular basis and occasionally had sex. Hinton knew that he could get along very well on his current path. But somehow, it was not enough.

What he really wanted was something like the first several years with Linda: romance, companionship, a shared life, someone to sleep with and, of course, good sex. He wanted it all, not just parts of it. One of his favorite memories was the day he and Linda met by accident. He remembered every detail. It was genuinely an accident. Hinton was riding his newly acquired bicycle into the parking lot at Carole's – a combination laundromat, bar, and bookstore that had become an Austin institution. What could be a better business near a major university?

He was headed towards a bike rack when Linda backed out of a parking space and hit the front wheel of his bike. His natural instinct was to be angry, but when Linda got out of the car and approached him, the only thing he could do was to drop his jaw and stare. She was beautiful

141

and the first words out of her mouth were "Are you hurt? I'll pay to have your bike fixed." After Hinton reassured her that he was unhurt and they had exchanged names and phone numbers, he said: "There is a bike shop just down the street. It is only a couple of blocks. I will take it there and let you know what happens." Then Linda said "I'll go with you in case you need a ride home and really, I will pay." At the shop, they left the bike which would be ready the next day. Linda offered to buy him lunch at any place he wanted. Surprised, Hinton told her that he lived only another block or two away. They walked to his rented duplex on Speedway, now a church parking lot, and got in his jeep. Linda said, "Anywhere you want to go."

Hinton headed to Sarah's on Balcones Drive. While the neighborhood was upscale, Sarah's place was little more than a shack with a grill and ice-cold beer. Before they could sit down at the bar, Sarah set an ice cold Lone Star longneck on the bar and had a burger on the grill for Hinton. Sarah asked, "What does your girlfriend want?" Hinton reacted quickly: "Sarah, Linda is not my girlfriend. We just met an hour ago." Sarah, sometimes a grumpy old woman, replied. "Maybe I know something you don't".

As always, the burgers were good. The company was better. Hinton and Linda spent the rest of the afternoon at Sarah's getting to know each other. They were rarely apart after that. Six months later they got married. The piece of paper was not too important to either of them at the time. It was just easier than explaining their relationship to landlords and others. Sarah had been right.

Hinton dozed off for a while realizing that nothing like that could be reconstructed. He thought about Millie for a while. What was he trying to do with Millie? They had shared a lot together. Millie was always there when needed. She had helped raise his daughter and he had done the same for her. There was not much they did not share except the bedroom. Sex was still taboo. Millie made that clear in Paris. Linda had also warned Hinton that Millie wanted nothing to do with a change in their relationship. No sex. No marriage. Just friends she had said. Give it up and find someone else. Maybe he should. Besides, he had other things to deal with on the train.

He fell asleep again for what seemed like only a few minutes. The conductor woke him up and informed him that they were pulling into Geneva and that he would need to change trains for Paris. Conductors are very useful people when they want to be.

Hinton had most of an hour before his next train would leave. Carrying his duffle bag and backpack, he walked outside for a few minutes. He questioned why he took the train in the first place. It was the middle of the night. The outside air felt good, and his mood brightened. A cabbie offered him a lift into town, which he declined. After he finished talking to the cabbie, he was startled. He was almost positive that the woman he had seen entering the station was the mystery woman. After some thought he dismissed the idea. No matter how good the mystery woman might be at following someone, she could not have done so this evening. She was not at the airport in Vienna. She was not on the train. No one, except Johnston and Linda, knew what he was doing. Neither one of them would have divulged his itinerary to anyone else—especially not to the mystery woman. He convinced himself that he was sleep deprived and imagining things. He bought a large coffee and two croissants from the one café open all night and headed to the platform. He felt relief to get back on the train and settle in for the next part of his journey. He knew what he would think about.

The most pressing thing to deal with was the mess of two murders and a pending crisis in the oil industry. Was his job done? Ross had been found and interviewed by Johnston. Finding Ross was all he had agreed to do. He had not promised to solve the murders or to stabilize world oil markets. These tasks were probably beyond his capabilities in any case. They were, as the saying goes, above his pay grade. Still, his curiosity and his respect for Patti Walker might keep him involved. He decided to think about all this in the same way he approached most problems. He would analyze the situation systematically and with an open mind. What was his goal, objective, endgame? That was easy. He wanted to extricate himself from all forms of cloak and dagger work, go back to Norman, take Fergie for long walks, and resume his academic career.

Hinton knew that the place to start was to look at the major players in the oil game, the individual suspects in the murder cases could wait. Someone or some group was financing these shenanigans. If he could figure who was putting up the cash, he could probably figure out who was causing the trouble. There were too many players in the game to sort them all out individually. Oil companies, at least the major producers, were all good candidates. Many of them had well-deserved reputations for being less than good citizens. In much of the world, oil is produced by nations or national companies, and these too should be on the list of possible financiers.

Hinton asked himself the obvious question: who would benefit most from derailing a Saudi shift to greener energy? Phrasing the question differently he asked who would be hurt the most if the Saudi plan were implemented. Hinton's answer surprised even him. If the Saudis announced that they were going green and would steadily reduce oil production, oil producers in general would see short term gains from higher prices. Some of them might even see increased demand to meet global needs for oil.

Besides, many oil companies were at least paying lip service to the

144

transition and recognizing that climate change was real. Nearly all of them seemed committed to end flaring of natural gas and to reduce methane emissions from their operations. Some like BP were doing more than that. BP agreed to install EV charging stations in China. Shell was investing heavily in wind and solar. These firms know that the transition will happen and that they can make money from it. Many are agnostic about where the money comes from. The majors still spend plenty of money on political donations around the world and on lobbying efforts. Still, none of the oil companies seemed likely to be involved in murder or other crimes over this issue.

Hinton concluded that the most likely culprits were nations. It occurred to him that the Russians might be involved. Yes, they would welcome higher prices because oil and gas were about the only things bringing in foreign currency in a faltering economy. They needed foreign exchange earnings to pay for imports. Why would they object to the Saudis intentions to go green? The answer might be as simple as one word: Putin.

The Russian leader had never really liked the idea of joining the Saudis to form OPEC+. He did not like MBS personally or the arrogance of the Saudi leaders. Russia was a junior partner in this endeavor and the Saudis made that clear. It was at least plausible that Putin was just having some fun at the expense of the Saudis or seeking revenge for the way he had been treated. What Putin seems to want is power and influence. Anything he might accomplish that would damage the power and influence of the Saudis might be a good thing in his eyes. Putin does not need to be rational. He has a long history of doing things that would be regarded by most analysts as irrational. Besides, there were other actors in Russia. Hinton placed Russia, at least for the time-being, on the top of his list.

What other nations could be behind all this? The Iranians could certainly finance a lot of trouble and had done so in the past. They were not friends of the Saudis. The Iranian leadership was determined not to let the Saudis dominate the region politically or economically. There were also religious differences with the Saudis that could not be tolerated. In the recent past, the Iranians had been accused of various attempts at sabotage in the Kingdom. And the Houthi attacks on the Saudi refineries were probably financed by Iran even if the drones did not take off from Iranian territory as many people thought. Hinton discounted the possibility that the Iranians were responsible for the murders. The Iranians had been involved in many terrorist activities and always denied their involvement. Still, there was always some sign that they had done the deed. No, it was not likely to be Iran.

Hinton quickly dismissed Libya as the culprit. They had been involved in a lot of nasty acts, including the bombing of PanAm flight 103 over Scotland. The problem with the Libyans was that they really had no organized government since the Arab Spring and the death of Qaddafi. Years later, they were still fighting among themselves for control of the country and its oil exports. They were probably not capable of conducting operations on two continents.

In a similar fashion, Hinton dismissed Nigeria. That poor nation had a lot of oil, a lot of corruption, and more internal conflicts than you could count, raging inflation, and widespread poverty. Between Boko Haram, the Niger Delta River group, and political instability, Nigeria could probably be counted out.

Venezuela had plenty at stake, but the Madero regime was facing difficulties as bad as those in Nigeria if not Libya. The most likely national government involvement came from Russia. But there was another possibility. There are wealthy and powerful people in Saudi

Arabia who have dedicated their lives to the oil industry. One or more of them could be acting on their own to sabotage the energy transition. That would be a very dangerous game to play but not impossible. If the transition threatened their power and prestige, who knows? The question would be who would dare to try to do this.

Hinton understood that the more important events were those in the energy markets, not the two murders. He also understood that unraveling the murder stories depended on linking individual suspects to one or more of the major players in the energy world. He spent some time thinking about the possible suspects and their connections. He reminded himself to keep an open mind. This meant that the killer or killers might not even be on his list.

Hinton started with Ross. After all, it was Ross who got him involved in this business. Johnston and the Agency would not have approached him except for Ross. Clearly, Ross was still on their list. Despite the interviews with Ross and his denials, as well as a lack of evidence, Ross was the last known person to have been with Patti Walker before her gruesome death. Hinton remained doubtful that Ross had the nerves or ability to have been the killer. He did not know if Ross had serious connections to the major players in the game, but it was entirely possible. Ross certainly knew a lot of people in the industry. Hinton concluded that Ross must stay on the list.

An obvious suspect was the mystery woman. She seemed to be everywhere. She had been in DC, London, Paris, and Vienna. No one had been able to identify her. The mystery woman's motives were unclear unless she were a paid assassin. Hinton knew that most killers were men, but he told himself to keep an open mind. This woman certainly knew the art of disguise, how to follow someone, and how to avoid being interviewed by the authorities. Since her background was unknown, Hinton had no idea of her skills that might allow her to become a killer. The Agency was spending a lot of effort in their failed attempts to identify her. What bothered Hinton the most, of course, was that the mystery woman was apparently following him. Was he next on her list? Hinton did not know, but he knew to keep her on his list.

Keeping an open mind meant that Hinton had to consider the possibility that the murders were an Agency operation. Could Johnston have committed one or both murders? Johnston was in DC at the time of Patti Walker's murder. He was in London when Diane Stoddard was killed. If Johnston did not kill Patti Walker, he certainly would have known enough of the details to commit a similar crime in London. But why? Did the Agency have its own agenda that they were not disclosing? Could Johnston have decided to do it on his own? Hinton did not trust Johnston and thought it was possible that he was involved. He must keep Johnston on his list.

Then came the most difficult part. He had to consider the possibility that the Rabbi was somehow involved. Other than Millie and Linda, the Rabbi was his closest personal friend. He trusted the Rabbi completely. They had been friends since graduate school in Austin. The Rabbi had taken him on the trip to Riyadh and then warned him to leave immediately. On the other hand, the Rabbi's entire career was wrapped up in oil and gas. Even graduate school at UT was an oil and gas decision for the Rabbi. Could he be doing something on his own? Could he be acting on orders from someone higher up? Oddly, the Rabbi was in both DC and London at the time of the murders. Hinton was confident that the Rabbi had not personally committed the murders. Could he have facilitated the murders in some fashion? The possibility gnawed at Hinton's mind, but he had to consider it.

Considering what he thought was impossible, Hinton turned his thoughts to Rose, the LSE student. She had admitted to being in DC at a conference when Patti Walker was killed. She had returned to London in plenty of time for Diane Stoddard's death. Hinton knew very little about her background except that she was from an oil producing country. What was her age? She could have been anywhere in her twenties. Was she as innocent as her bright smile and cheerful greetings suggested? Hinton did not know. He was not even certain that he wanted to find out. If she was not who she pretended to be, Hinton's ability to judge other people in any circumstance would be shattered.

Hinton had another glass of wine and fell asleep to the comfortable sounds of the train. He woke up when the train slowed down as it was entering Paris. Despite his love of trains, Hinton was ready to leave. It had been a 20-hour trip from Vienna and he looked forward to some food and a real bed. Once again, he checked into the Gare du Nord Hotel. Since he was not in a rush to get to London, he could spend a day or two if he liked in Paris. He ate at the hotel restaurant which turned out to be a very good choice.

Coffee and croissants were all he needed the next morning. As he walked through the lobby after this quick breakfast, he spotted the mystery woman. He became alert immediately. His curiosity about her identity was intense. This time he decided to turn the tables on her. He decided to follow her just to see where she would go. Maybe she would recognize that she was being tailed and he could confront her.

Hinton had not followed anyone since his early days at the Agency. Doing so successfully required serious training and practice. He had once had the training, but he knew that practice counted for a lot. He would not even think of a serious handball match without being in practice. Why should he think he could pull this off?

The mystery woman did not seem to be in a hurry and did not seem to notice that she was being followed. Hinton followed her to Montmartre where she casually looked at paintings offered by street artists. She bought a cup of coffee and after some searching found a bench to sit on. Hinton did not think she had noticed him. She seemed not to have a care in the world.

From Montmartre the mystery woman walked south towards Place de Bastille and then crossed the river and headed for the Sorbonne. This journey seemed like a long walk, but it was only a little over three miles. Hinton was glad that she was a walker. She would almost certainly notice him on public transport. Hinton was careful to stay at least 50 feet behind her and take precautions in case she turned around. So far, she had given no sign of recognizing him or taking any evasive actions.

She walked around the grounds of the Sorbonne and stopped to talk to two people who appeared to be faculty members. From a distance, Hinton could tell that they knew her and were pleased to run into her. A few minutes later she stopped to talk to another person who also seemed to be a faculty member. For some reason she stopped in one of the pathways near some bushes and just looked for a while. She looked as if the place had some special significance. Hinton made the obvious conclusion that the mystery woman had at one time or another been a student at the Sorbonne. When he got a chance, he would ask the Rabbi if he had ever met such a woman while he was a student there.

The mystery woman then walked for a while in the nearby Luxembourg gardens and then crossed the river and walked the length of the Champs-Elysées, only slightly more than a mile long. She window shopped but bought nothing. She stopped at a café and bought a coffee and a croissant. Hinton followed her past the Arc de Triomphe and into the nearby Bois de Boulogne, where she sat down on the nearest bench. Within a few seconds, a young man, probably from the Middle East, sat down on the bench. They did not engage in conversation.

The young man got up and walked away within a minute or two after stooping down to tie his shoes. When he left, the mystery woman opened an envelope which he had left beside her on the bench. She removed some cash and placed it in her small handbag. Then she removed a cell phone from the envelope and pushed a single button on the phone. She talked for only a minute or two, mostly listening. When she hung up, she removed the SIMM card from the phone and with her scarf cleaned off her fingerprints. Later, she would ditch the phone, envelope, and SIMM card in different trash bins.

Hinton could not retrieve any of these items without being obvious, so he continued to follow her. She again walked the length of the Champs-Elysées to its end at Place de la Concorde, where much to Hinton's surprise, she entered the metro station. Hinton followed her to a crowded platform and stood far enough away to get on a separate car. Just as the train was arriving, the mystery woman walked towards Hinton and before boarding, she said: "Good afternoon, Mr. Hinton. Good luck. You will need it." Stunned, Hinton did not board the train and gave up his attempt to follow her.

Chapter 14

London Again

Back at the Hotel du Nord, Hinton had an early dinner, several glasses of wine, and contemplated what he had learned by following the mystery woman. Tomorrow, he would take the Eurostar to London but after a long day walking all over Paris, he would not go out for a night on the town. What he really wanted was a chicken fried steak and he renewed his vow to search for the best chicken fried steak in Texas.

Hinton had learned a lot about the mystery woman. Obviously, she knew who he was. When she spoke to him, she called him by name. She was clearly not afraid of him. She made no effort to evade his surveillance. She was communicating with someone in a clandestine fashion. Was she receiving instructions on what to do next? More than likely this connection had ties to the Middle East. But where? She was probably a former student at the Sorbonne. The faculty members who stopped to talk to her were pleased to see her.

Hinton texted the Rabbi to ask if he knew such a person. He gave the Rabbi as complete a description as possible but as expected, the Rabbi said the description was not enough. The photo of the mystery woman Hinton had taken at dinner with Millie in Paris was of no help to the Rabbi. Did the Rabbi know if there was a photo archive at the Sorbonne that could be searched? Yes, but it is restricted to former and current students, faculty, and staff. Hinton thanked the Rabbi. No doubt Johnston and his friends could find a way to search the Sorbonne archives. Hinton thought he could recognize one or two of the faculty members who had talked to the mystery woman.

The next morning Hinton would not have been surprised to see either the mystery woman, Johnston, or both in the hotel restaurant. Neither one was there. Hinton took his time with his coffee and croissant and noticed in the *Financial Times* that the price of Brent and West Texas Intermediate (WTI) had spiked by more than $10 per barrel overnight. The usual comedians (analysts) offered no explanation other than a drop in US crude inventories. Hinton knew that was not the whole story. A couple of calls to his industry friends would clear that up, but Hinton was more interested in purchasing a Eurostar ticket.

Hinton took the 10 am Eurostar from Gare du Nord to London. Since this was his second ride on the Eurostar, Hinton felt like a regular. He still did not like the Eurostar as much as other trains. It was too fast to enjoy the countryside. The main advantage, he decided, was that two and a half hours to London from Paris was as fast as flying, at least if you included travel time to airports and waiting to get on the plane.

When he arrived at St. Pancras, he checked into the adjoining Great Northern Hotel. The hotel was an old one but more upscale than the New Premier Inn. The Great Northern had a highly rated restaurant, two bars, a coffee shop and advertised itself as a full-service hotel. The room was very pleasant, and Hinton was more than satisfied with his choice despite the high price. After long hours on the train and his disturbing thoughts about what might happen next, what Hinton really wanted was a massage. He did not want one of the many so-called massage parlors, which were, for the most part, thinly disguised whorehouses. He really wanted a massage. He looked in the binder describing hotel services and found just what he was looking for. He called and made an appointment for 2 pm.

The masseuse was a young woman from Bangladesh who introduced herself as Siri. Hinton smiled, very confident that Siri was not her real name. Hinton did not care what her name might be. She was very professional and very good at what she did. After a couple of minutes, she told Hinton that his muscles were very tight and asked if he was under some kind of pressure. Hinton explained that he had been on a train for a long time and that he was facing both personal and professional challenges. Siri said he had come to the right place. She promised that when he left, he and his muscles would be more relaxed than he had ever known. They barely spoke after that. Siri went back to work and Hinton soon forgot about everything else except the tender but sometimes firm pressure of Siri's hands.

An hour and a half later Siri said that he should be in good shape. Hinton was pleased. All tension seemed to be gone. He put on his clothes, signed the bill charging the massage to his room, and gave Siri a very large tip. He did not care that the massage had cost him more than the price of the room. It was worth every penny. Hinton promised himself a return visit after his LSE lecture the next day.

He walked the three blocks to the pub where he had met Johnston before. One of the small outside tables was available and Hinton sat down. In less than a minute, the waiter brought him a pint and asked if he wanted to wait for his friend before ordering food. Hinton said he preferred to wait, but after an hour, Johnston was still a no-show. That was okay with Hinton. He had made no specific arrangements with Johnston. The waiter brought him another pint without asking and this time he also brought fish and chips. Hinton had become a regular at the pub. Before leaving, he checked oil prices from an app on his phone. In the last three days both Brent and WTI prices had spiked more than $30 per barrel, then dropped by more than $40 per barrel the next day. Hinton

155

expected this volatility to continue.

Hinton left the pub and headed down the street to Pret a Manger. He knew that this was not the time of day that Rose would be there, but he wanted to confirm that. As expected, there was no sign of Rose. Next he walked to the Tavistock Hotel where he was almost certain to run into Sadiq.

When he walked into the lobby, Sadiq said, "If you are still looking for your friend Ross, I have not seen him but both the man and woman who had been searching for Ross came by earlier in the day."

Hinton thanked Sadiq and left. No tip this time, but Sadiq did not seem to expect one.

Back on the street walking to his hotel, Hinton thought it was odd that the mystery woman and Johnston had both been searching for Ross again. Johnston had already interviewed Ross in Vienna. Why would he still be looking for Ross? If he wanted to keep tabs on Ross, he could have had him followed. He was at more of a loss to explain the mystery woman's interest in Ross. Some things would just remain unknown, and Hinton did not like that.

At the hotel, Hinton had another pint and returned to his room. He was still relaxed from the massage but knew that he should get a good night's sleep before his lecture. Before he could get to sleep, Millie called and after a brief greeting she got to the point,

"You owe me big-time. The last of the fake social media posts have been taken down and our IT folks will watch to make certain that nothing reappears."

"Thank you, Millie. I always owe you big time. What else is happening?"

"I think you know Lloyd Brinkman, the chief of staff of the Senate Energy and Natural Resources Committee. Brinkman tried to find you on

156

campus but had no luck. He wants you to testify before the committee on Monday about the current volatility in oil prices. The other panelists will be chief executives from two large oil companies and the chief economist from the Department of Energy."

"Once upon a time, he had my cell number. What did you tell him?"

"I told him you would be there and that you would be happy to testify. I knew you would not turn down an opportunity like that."

"Millie, you know me too well. It will not be easy, but I will be there. Can you book a flight for me from Heathrow to Dulles on Saturday?"

"Consider it done. I will use your personal credit card for this one, but you can afford it."

A Saturday flight would give him a day in DC before his testimony. He did not ask Millie to get him a ticket to the Nationals - Astros game on Sunday. He would take care of that when he got there. His London lecture was scheduled for Thursday morning but there were other things for him to do before he could leave town. He wanted to talk to Johnston, Rose, and if possible, to Cindy Burgess. And he needed to shop for a tie. He would probably be okay before the Senate Committee with his sport coat in the summer, but a tie was essential.

Early Thursday morning he went to Pret. Rose was there and he ordered an omelet, a banana, and a large coffee. The place was crowded, and he had to wait until nearly 8 am before he could speak to Rose. He wanted to make certain that she was aware of his lecture at LSE and that she could attend. Rose smiled. She was way ahead of Hinton. She knew about the lecture and had already arranged time-off to attend. Management had been very supportive of her efforts to take classes and participate in university events. Hinton told Rose that he would return to talk to her about the doctoral program at OU.

157

Hinton walked to LSE, a journey of just more than a mile. He liked LSE. Who could not like a university founded by George Bernard Shaw and Beatrice Webb. Technically, LSE was the London School of Economics and Political Science, but it was commonly known as the London School of Economics. It was a major part of the larger University of London system. Hinton liked the campus. From the outside, it appeared to be just a bunch of old buildings. Inside it was a modern, well-equipped campus equipped with the most recent technology.

Hinton found the office of his friend Lowell Smith-Thompson after a few minutes of searching. Smith-Thompson's office had been moved since his last visit.

Lowell grinned at the sight of Hinton and began the conversation. "Good to see you my friend and thanks much for agreeing to give a lecture. The students really like to hear from people outside LSE."

"I will do my best to entertain them. They seem like students at OU. Something different from listening to the same old faculty day after day is a relief. What have you been doing since our last encounter?"

"Sadly, administrative work seems to have taken over my life. I need to do something about that or go crazy. And you?"

"I don't seem to have worn out my welcome at OU and I have been publishing a bit. Before you ask, Linda and I got a divorce. I know you always enjoyed being around her, but we are probably both better off as a result. I still talk to her often and we remain good friends."

"I am sorry to hear about your divorce. I always thought your marriage would last until death do us part. I hate to change the subject, but we should wander down to the lecture hall. We scheduled the central auditorium for our distinguished visitor. Do you mind if we record the lecture so that people who could not attend can view it?"

"I have no objections at all. I am honored that you think others might want to see it."

"You might be surprised and at least, you are here unlike your friend Ross who was supposed to be at a round-table last week."

Although they were a few minutes early, the lecture hall was already filling up. Hinton and Smith-Thompson took seats on the stage to the right of the podium. Hinton took the opportunity to glance at the crowd. He almost immediately noticed Johnston in the back row. Two or three rows down he was pleased to see Rose but thought it was nice to have some familiar faces in the crowd. Then on the front row, he saw the mystery woman. Sitting next to her was a woman that he would later learn was Cindy Burgess. The two women did not seem to know each other. At least they were not carrying on a conversation.

Smith-Thompson introduced Hinton with biographical details that made him sound more important than he really was. Hinton was a bit embarrassed, but he was still relaxed and looking forward to the next hour or two. He loved a good audience and he had learned a few tricks about capturing an audience's attention. Although he never lectured from notes, he always carried a file folder to the podium and opened it. He had learned long ago that having something that looked like a prepared lecture on the podium sent a message that he was organized and had prepared for the event. It was an effective strategy. He also picked out two or three people in the audience that he could make eye contact with. These were the people he watched for reactions.

Hinton's lecture went exactly as he had planned it on the train from Vienna, but he opened with a story he had heard many times in Austin. When Lyndon Johnson was president, he was scheduled to address the National Education Association (the teachers union) and he called in a speech writer to prepare his remarks. A couple of days later the speech

159

writer returned with a draft. Lyndon read the first page and told the writer to get the hell out of his office and bring him a speech worthy of the event. After two more days, the writer returned with a second draft. Again, the president rejected the speech and gave the writer some ideas on what he wanted to say. The time for the speech was fast approaching and the next day the writer appeared in the oval office with a third draft. This time the president read the first page and said he was delighted, but he did not read beyond the first page. On the day of the speech the president got through the first page. When he turned to the second page there were only two lines:"You are on your own now, Mr. President. I quit." In truth, Hinton admitted, the writer had used a somewhat more vulgar phrase than "Mr. President." The audience loved it and Hinton knew that he could tell his tales of scandal in the oil and gas industry to a friendly audience. His next words were: "So I guess I am on my own now." This brought additional laughter.

The Q&A after Hinton's lecture was also fun. The first question was from a student who asked: "Was the story about President Johnston true and if so, what was the vulgar phrase used by the speech writer?" Hinton replied that the story was more than likely true and though he did not want to say the words in public, the letters "mf" might help to decode the vulgarity. There was laughter all around.

The second question was from another student who asked, "What should we be studying if we wanted to become experts on the oil and gas industry?" Hinton replied: "A little bit of economics as long as you don't take the fairy tales about competitive markets and equilibrium that you were taught as undergraduates too seriously. The world does not operate that way. You should also take courses in accounting, finance, geology, law, and international relations. If you can't read financial statements, you have no chance of understanding the industry. If you don't know

160

some basic geology, conversations with industry people will be nearly impossible." Surprisingly, the student seemed pleased with the answer.

The Q&A session continued for a while but eventually the crowd dwindled to just a few people including Johnston and Cindy Burgess. Hinton agreed to meet Johnston the next day at 4 pm at the usual place. Cindy Burgess introduced herself and Hinton immediately asked if she would like to have lunch. Smith-Thompson excused himself to attend a department meeting. Hinton and Burgess did not know each other but they knew of each other. They were comfortable almost immediately. The two would spend the rest of the afternoon together.

Hinton mentioned the murders of Patti Walker and Diane Stoddard. Cindy had been working with both. She was very disturbed by their deaths and remained so. She was at a loss for the motivations. Cindy said the embassy was providing 24/7 security for her and that this was a serious invasion of her private life. She had learned to live with it. Visitors were permitted if the security detail had been notified in advance. A couple of times she had managed to sneak out of the house without them knowing.

Cindy updated Hinton on some of her work. She was working on a new model of the oil and gas industry. It was a substantially different model from the Department of Energy modeling system known as NEMS (National Energy Modeling System), which is more than three decades old. NEMS had been modified over the years, but it is awkward to use and written in FORTRAN, a language most potential users don't know.

Cindy explained that the new model would be a systems dynamics model based on stocks, flows, and feedback loops. Unlike NEMS, the new model would have a user-friendly interface, something any twelve-year-old or the most computer illiterate member of Congress could use

161

with ease. Importantly, the new model called GEMS (Global Energy Modeling System) would incorporate international oil and gas production and demand in a meaningful way. The model even incorporated the latest theories of international relations to model potential political unrest. Cindy laughed and said: "The first time I ran the model, I started World War III."

Hinton and Burgess continued talking for several hours. The two energy analysts could have talked for days. It is no easy task to try to sort out what is going on with energy markets. Climate change, the energy transition, political shenanigans, and technological change were as important as traditional issues of supply and demand.

The conversation turned to vulnerabilities of the energy system. They agreed that the electric grid almost anywhere was vulnerable to natural disasters and sabotage. They laughed at the outages in Texas during the most recent freeze and why ERCOT (Electric Reliability Council of Texas) refused to join the national grid so that they could draw power from elsewhere during emergencies. And, as California had demonstrated, taking out a sub-station or two could create havoc for several days or even weeks.

They also discussed the vulnerabilities created by the geographic concentration of refining capacity in the US and Europe. In the US, 60 percent of refining capacity was concentrated in a small region along the Gulf Coast from Houston to New Orleans. Direct hits by hurricanes could create huge shortages. So could drone attacks. The US had been lucky in the past but there were no guarantees that this would not happen. All anyone needed to look at was the price spike in California when two refineries went off-line for maintenance at the same time. The good news was that the computer systems used by refineries were not connected to the internet, as was the case with nuclear power plants. There was simply no possibility that they could be hacked and put out of service except from the inside.

Pipelines were a different story. A US natural gas pipeline company had just paid $10 million in crypto currency to hackers in a ransomware attack. The company had no way to get their control systems operational without paying the ransom. Cindy said that another way to cause mischief was just to take control of the pipeline computer systems. A lot more damage could be done that way. She said it was not difficult to do and offered to demonstrate it for Hinton, who declined the offer. He already knew how to do it. Why the pipeline companies did not have duplicate computer systems in different locations like banks, insurance companies and the Federal Reserve System was beyond their comprehension. Yes, it was expensive to maintain back-up systems but much cheaper than paying ransom money or having the entire pipeline system crash.

Supertankers were too difficult to damage enough to make them good targets and they could avoid natural disasters such as hurricanes. Nuclear generating facilities were not good targets either. Several feet of reinforced concrete and steel made them almost impermeable to terrorist attacks. Human error and stupid designs, such as building Fukushima in the wrong place were possible, but no one outside of Chernobyl had ever been killed by a nuclear generating plant.

They discussed the possibility of a coordinated attack on many types of energy facilities around the world or in a single country. Could it be done? The possibility was very remote and to carry out such attacks simultaneously could only be done by a nation-state. Even then, the number of people involved would be large and people talk. No, that was not likely.

They finished their discussion of vulnerability and eventually, the conversation returned to Ross. Burgess liked Ross, undoubtedly more than Hinton did. She told Hinton much the same story she had told Johnston of her encounter with Ross. They had dinner and discussed the oil industry. Then they went to a club, but she did not say that it was the BDSM Society. She then left to be with her lover. Ross had not done anything out of the ordinary and she had no reason to fear him. She hoped to continue their conversations.

When they finally looked at the clock, it was well after 6 pm. Hinton asked if they could continue their conversation over dinner. Cindy said she had a prior commitment and could not. They agreed to meet again whenever they were in the same city. They had become good friends in only an afternoon. As Cindy got up to leave, Hinton noticed the security guard who had been not far away the whole time. He was glad security had been provided for Cindy but scolded himself for not having identified the man earlier.

Hinton returned to the hotel, called and was lucky enough to reserve another massage with Siri. He had an early dinner, took a short walk, and kept his massage appointment. He needed the massage and was grateful for Siri's professional hands. He had a lot to do the next day. Among other things he needed to figure out what to tell the Senate Committee. They would expect a written statement but that was more and more unlikely. That is their problem, Hinton mused. They invited me on short notice while I was out of the country. He could always submit his written statement later.

Friday morning, he went straight to Pret a Manger for breakfast. His real purpose, of course, was to talk Rose into graduate school at OU. He knew this was a risky venture. The last graduate student he had recruited was an utter failure. The young man dropped out after not completing his first semester. That's how it works sometimes. He thought Rose had the ability and desire to complete a doctoral program. He could handle the risk of student failure. What he was more concerned about was the possibility that Rose was somehow involved in this mess. She was from an energy producing country. She had been in DC and London for both murders. Her student status could be just for visa purposes and it was a good cover. Who would suspect a young Nigerian woman of committing such crimes? If this were the case, Hinton admitted to himself, he was a terrible judge of character.

Hinton had to wait until break time to talk to Rose. He knew that would be the case when he arrived at 7 am. That was fine with Hinton. He read the morning papers and was a bit disturbed that oil and gas price instability was still going on. He was not surprised but was more disturbed that broader financial markets had also become highly volatile. The major stock market indices were all down only a day after they had been sharply up. Was it possible that the movers and shakers on Wall Street, London, and Tokyo knew something that he did not know? Not likely. If that were the case, it would have been reported somewhere.

On page 3 of the business section of the London Times, a short article caught Hinton's attention. Yesterday, there were small explosions at oil storage facilities in New Orleans, Rotterdam, Istanbul, and Karachi. The explosions caused little damage except in Karachi where an oil storage tank had been penetrated and several thousand gallons of crude were spilled on the ground. The most disturbing part of the article was that, despite time zone differences, the explosions occurred at the same time. Authorities in the four cities had no suspects but did report that the explosive devices had similar characteristics.

Hinton understood immediately that this was the work of a very sophisticated organization. More than likely, the explosions were test runs or a demonstration that simultaneous attacks could occur. Oil

165

storage tanks are enormous containers that can hold as much as a million barrels of oil. If the explosives had been placed carefully, four or five percent of a day's global consumption of crude could have been destroyed.

While Hinton was pondering who could have been behind these attacks, Rose sat down at his table for her break. She appeared happy to see Hinton and began to talk,

"I really enjoyed your lecture at LSE. Great fun."

"Thank you. I am glad it did not bore you. I really want to talk to you about the PhD program at OU. I think you would be a good fit. Do you want to give it a try?"

"I would love to do that. I do want to complete a doctorate. Sadly, I don't think I can do that financially. I don't have the money and my parents have spent a lot on my LSE studies. Even with a full scholarship covering tuition and fees, there are other expenses I don't have the money for. Even with the graduate assistantship you talked about, I don't have the money for transportation or living expenses for the first month or two before I start to get paid."

"I understand. Although it is unusual to provide transportation subsidies for graduate students, I will arrange it."

"That would be wonderful."

"I will be back in touch with specifics."

Hinton did not know how he was going to arrange it but he would find a way to do it even if it meant writing a check himself. Rose was more than pleased and said that she had completed the on-line application. Hinton would later call Millie, the fixer. If anyone could figure out how to get around university regulations it was Millie. He looked forward to having Rose in the program. It would be good for the other graduate students to have a colleague with a very different background.

Rose's break was soon finished, and Hinton left Pret a Manger. He had agreed to meet Johnston at 4 pm at the pub. In the meantime, he would try to figure out what to tell the Senate Committee. He welcomed a few hours to think.

A few minutes before 4 o'clock Hinton sat down at one of the outside tables at the pub. He thought it was odd that the pub did not have a colorful name as was the tradition for English pubs. This one simply said Euston Street Pub on the sign. If he got a chance, he would ask the waiter about it. He did not really have a chance as Johnston arrived within a minute or two and with no greeting began talking,

"We have a lot to talk about."

"Then let's get started. I don't have a lot of time today."

"Deuce wants you to stop by Langley on your way back to Oklahoma."

"That won't be a problem. I have agreed to testify before the Senate Energy and Natural Resources Committee on Monday."

"I am aware of the committee meeting, but I did not know that you were going to testify. I don't think they can do much of anything to smooth out the current situation, but it is a good thing you agreed to do it."

"I didn't know either until a few hours ago."

Abruptly, Johnston changed the subject,

"The FBI and the DC police are convinced that Ross killed Patti Walker. They don't have enough evidence yet to charge him. Juries take the phrase 'beyond a reasonable doubt' very seriously these days. We are also convinced that Ross is guilty. After much searching, the DC police found video from a store on Connecticut Avenue showing someone who looked like Ross walking in the direction of the Wardman about an hour after Ross said Patti dropped him off at the Wardman. The cameras in the Wardman parking lot show Ross getting into his rental car. They do not show him getting out of another car. The timing of the videos indicates that Ross was not telling the truth about his activities that night. And since Ross freely admits that he was at the party in Crystal City with Patti, there are no other probable suspects."

Hinton interrupted. "But they still have no physical or forensic evidence that Ross was ever in Patti's house?"

"Yes, that is correct and that is why they have not arrested him."

Hinton was not satisfied with that answer and pressed Johnston. "What possible motive could Ross have for killing Patti in such a brutal fashion, or at all? Was Ross some sort of sexual deviant who had suddenly decided to become a killer? If so, why is there nothing in his previous activities to suggest anything was wrong with him? How could a man in his late forties suddenly transform himself into a monster? Did Johnston or anyone else know of anything like this in the past? "

"There have been other killers as old as Ross who had led seemingly normal lives with no evidence of prior activity that would cause them to be on anyone's suspect list. I don't have the psychological expertise to explain it."

As for motive, Johnston continued, "Large sums of money were deposited in bank accounts in Luxembourg and the Cayman Islands in accounts traced to Ross. The deposits occurred just before and just after Patti's murder. Ross has not attempted to access these accounts."

Again, Hinton interrupted. "This is preposterous. Do you really think that Ross is a hired killer? You have met him. He does not have the balls to do this."

"What else would anyone pay Ross to do? We know he has consulted with various oil companies and governments in the past, but

168

this is a lot more money than he has ever made on such jobs. He was paid a million dollars in accounts that he tried to hide. He is not just trying to beat the Internal Revenue Service. He didn't want anyone to know about this."

"A million dollars is not nearly enough even though it is probably ten times his annual salary. Risking everything for a mere million dollars does not make sense. Who traced the money to Ross and how was it done?"

Johnston was silent for a minute and then said, "I can't tell you how this was done or what agency did it. Doing so might jeopardize future operations. It doesn't matter that you have been working on this with us. It doesn't matter that Deuce trusts you. I just can't do it."

Hinton was not sure he should even be hearing this stuff and he was more than a little skeptical. "How do you expect me to believe this if you won't tell me how you got the information? None of it makes sense. And, then there is the question of why he would have committed such a brutal murder. There are many ways to kill someone that are much easier than the way Patti was killed. Even Ross could figure that out. I am not an expert, but it seems to me that the method used here would be much harder to do than just shooting her or stabbing her with a knife."

"We thought about that and the best we came up with was that he was trying to make it look like a sexual attack to cover his tracks."

The expression on Hinton's face made it clear that this explanation was not convincing.

Johnston continued. "We want you to be very careful. For all we know, you could be next on the list. Two energy analysts are dead, and we have good reason to believe that Ross is working for the Russians. We know that he visited Moscow and St. Petersburg two years ago. While there he met with executives from Gazprom and they seemed to get along very well. Ross took other trips to Russia as well. And there is more. Ross went to the offices of London Energy Consultants (LEC) more than once, including when he was in London recently. We did not find that out until after he left to go to Vienna, but we had been watching LEC for a while. It is nothing more than a front for Gazprom and Lukoil."

"So what? It is not against the law to consult with Russians, even directly. And that does not mean that the Russians hired him to be a killer. Besides, the trip Ross took to Russia was sponsored by the National Science Foundation to promote collaborative work between the two nations. And Ross has no particular expertise at killing people. Why not hire someone who is experienced to do the job?"

"The Russians often hire people who might be called amateurs to do nasty things including murders. They think this might distance them from the deed and provide plausible deniability. They are often wrong but that doesn't seem to matter."

Hinton and Johnston agreed to disagree on Ross's involvement in the murders. There seemed to be nothing either one of them could do about it anyway. Before Hinton left, Johnston gave him two numbers to contact Deuce. The first was a direct line to Deuce's office. The second was Deuce's cell phone number. Cell phones are strictly prohibited at Langley. You must check them in when arriving, but after hours there were no restrictions. Johnston wished Hinton the best on his Senate testimony, and both left the pub. Hinton would later get much the same story from Deuce.

When Hinton got back to his hotel room, he noticed that the room had been searched. It was a professional job. His bag had been opened and the open bottle of shampoo had been spilled. There was not much else to search that belonged to Hinton, but it was obvious that the search had not been limited to his duffle bag. Fortunately, there was not anything worth finding in his duffle bag or his room. He had already returned the Glock and the Agency cell phone to Johnston. The remainder of his expense money was on his person. He did not have an address book or notes that might be useful to anyone. The main question on Hinton's mind was who would want to search anything he had. He thought he could eliminate the Agency. Johnston knew perfectly well what he had been given and what had been returned. Some puzzles are just not worth solving. Hinton would move on to more important things.

Chapter 15

DC Again

In the morning, Hinton had a full English breakfast at the hotel. He would have preferred a cup of coffee and croissant at Pret a Manger where he might run into Rose again, but he would be on a long flight and wanted to fill up before he headed to Heathrow. Hinton took the tube from Kings Cross station, adjacent to St. Pancras, to Heathrow. As usual, Heathrow was crowded, and he was glad that he checked in early. Heathrow has an impressive array of duty-free shops ranging from inexpensive ones selling cheap items to very expensive places. You could buy almost anything you wanted at these shops. Hinton found an upscale men's store and bought a new tie, the most expensive tie he had ever owned. He also purchased a bottle of forty-year-old single malt scotch. He was a bourbon drinker, but this brand was so smooth he could not resist.

Hinton spent nearly an hour in the duty-free shops, surprised at himself because he generally took no pleasure in shopping. He arrived at his gate just in time to hear the announcement of a two-hour delay before his flight would take off. There was no explanation of the delay, and the gate agent could not or would not give him any more information. Welcome to modern air transportation. He thought of his friend's admonition: if you have time to spare, go by air. Hinton laughed out loud thinking that airlines may be less transparent and more deceptive than MI5 or the CIA. In fact, he thought spy organizations could learn a thing or two from the airlines about concealing information. He found his way to a coffee shop and had a very good cup of strong black coffee and watched his fellow passengers for entertainment.

When his flight was finally called for boarding, there was still no explanation for the delay and the gate agents had no information either. The flight was not full, and he soon learned that the seat next to his was empty. Hinton was as happy as he could be on an airplane. More room to spread out and, even better, he would not need to make small talk with someone randomly assigned to the next seat by some computer algorithm. The cabin crew was cheerful and efficient. The attractive young woman assigned to business class, where Hinton was seated, made certain that he had plenty of food and drink. The flight itself was uneventful.

When Hinton arrived at Dulles, he cleared customs quickly, grabbed a shuttle to the Metro for a rather long ride to Union Station. There were many things wrong with the District of Columbia, but Union Station was not one of them. It was one of Hinton's favorite places. Union Station had several places to eat ranging from cheap fast food to gourmet meals. It had fascinating shops and a lot going on besides the arrival and departure of trains. Even locals found it to be a good place to visit.

He had booked a room at the Marriott Courtyard on 2nd Street, just a short walk from Union Station, and more importantly, a short walk to the Old Senate Office Building where his committee meeting would take place on Monday. Hinton pondered calling Deuce, but he did not. There was no need to have any distractions before his senate testimony. Instead, he took a long walk around the Capitol grounds, returned to Union Station for a light meal, and generally just tried to shake off the effects of jet lag and a long flight.

Sunday morning, he managed to buy a ticket to the Nationals-Astros game on row 6 just behind third base. Hinton wished that the Cubs were in town, but that was too much to ask. Baseball would be enough even though he had no favorite in the game. It was simply that baseball had always been his refuge from the rest of the world. There was something magical about the sounds and smells of a baseball game that might be better than trains. He was still angry with the Astros for their 2017 cheating scandal, but he had to admit that watching Justin Verlander pitch would be fun. The Nationals too had some good players. Max Scherzer was a great pitcher, but Hinton wondered who if anyone was worth $42 million.

Hinton did not like the Nationals Stadium. It struck him as being too modern and too harsh. But it was baseball, and the game did not disappoint. The Nationals won 1-0, with the only run not scored until the seventh inning. The Astros would not be happy but as Bart Giamatti, the one-time MLB Commissioner and former Professor of English at Yale, once said: "The game is designed to break your heart." Hinton thought that baseball was not the only game designed to break your heart. His love-life was not exactly what he wanted it to be.

After the game, he called Millie just to check in. The topic of their relationship did not come up during the call. Millie talked about events on campus and the difficulty of dealing with a broken washing machine. Hinton volunteered to fix the washing machine when he returned. He had learned over the years that he was an excellent handyman and could fix almost anything mechanical. Millie said there was a lot for him to do when he returned to campus, and she hoped he would do so soon. Hinton assured her that he missed campus and, a little embarrassed, he admitted that he missed her also. Millie wished him good luck with his testimony. She did not ask if he was doing anything else in DC.

Monday morning, Hinton returned to Union Station and found a good breakfast, read the *Washington Post*, and watched the crowd. He arrived at the Old Senate Office Building shortly after 9 am. He wanted nothing to do with being late for testimony before a Senate Committee. Passing through security sometimes took a while, even though the guards were polite and efficient. He went directly to the hearing room where he found Lloyd Brinkman, who was glad to see him. Hinton explained that he would provide a written statement later. Brinkman understood completely that the invitation had come late, and that Hinton had been in London. Still, Brinkman looked a little distraught and when Hinton asked why, he said "Senator Wilson is in a foul mood today. Don't expect an easy time during Q&A."

Hinton refused to let Brinkman's warning disturb him. He had been here before. This was his third appearance before the committee. The room was familiar to him and so was the atmosphere. This was nothing like his first experience testifying before a Senate committee. That first time, nearly a decade ago, he had been intimidated and lacked confidence that he should be in the room with several US Senators and a formidable panel of experts. When he was honest with himself, he was downright scared as a rookie. Still, he managed to get through it without embarrassing himself. He guessed that he had done alright since he had been invited back more than once. He would handle Senator Wilson no matter how hard the questioning was.

Gradually, the other panelists and more staffers wandered into the hearing room. He already knew Alex Greenwood, the chief economist at the Department of Energy. They had met at energy conferences in the past. Hinton respected Greenwood and fully understood the constraints he was under as a public official. If you value your job, there are some things you just can't say if you are speaking for an important government agency. You pay a price to be in the middle of the action and to have the

176

privilege of being underpaid. Hinton admired that.

The next panelist to enter the room was Joe Throckmorton, the CEO and major shareholder in Throckmorton Oil and Gas. Like many others in the oil industry, Joe was a third-generation oil man. He had inherited his stake in the company, but not until he had started at the bottom and worked for his father's company and others for nearly twenty years. Throckmorton Oil and Gas was an exploration and production company that drilled on their own land and sometimes for others. The firm operated mainly in the Eagle Ford in South Texas. They had briefly ventured into refinery ownership but had done so at the wrong time. The refinery crack, the spread between input costs and what they could get for the refined products, was at an all-time low. Joe had experienced good times and bad. He would be a good witness.

The second CEO entered the room dressed in what must have been a $3,000 suit and looked uncomfortable in his hand-crafted western boots. He was, however, the CEO of a major oil producing firm that did everything from drilling to retail operations. Hinton knew who he was but had never met him. He instantly disliked the man. Before Hinton was introduced to him, the CEO read a text message and called Brinkman aside. Later, Hinton learned that the CEO apologized and said that he must leave due to an emergency. He told Brinkman that everyone in town would know the nature of the emergency soon. Then he was gone. Hinton was relieved. The panel would still be a good one.

Just before 10 am, the room had become crowded with spectators and Hinton noted that there were eight Senators already seated. In most Senate Committee meetings only three or four Senators were present unless a vote was expected. There would be no vote today. The Senators, staffers and audience were there to listen to what was being said. They were puzzled and concerned about recent developments in the industry.

They wanted to see if there was some action Congress could take to settle things down.

Senator Wilson, the chair of the committee, called the meeting to order, introduced the panel, talked briefly about the rules of the committee, and asked for statements from each of the panelists, beginning with Alex Greenwood.

Greenwood was the ultimate professional, calm, diplomatic, and incredibly dull. He explained that the recent volatility in energy prices was a little unusual but hardly unprecedented. Nearly all economists, he maintained, would be at a loss to explain the price fluctuations. Economists will always tell you that there has been a change in either supply or demand or both. That is what we are trained to do. Anything else is outside the realm of economic science. Alex said the recent price volatility was not accompanied by corresponding changes in supply and demand.

Alex went on to say, correctly, that what had occurred in recent days was a change in expectations. Economists had understood for a long time that commodities, especially oil and gas, are bought and sold based on market expectations of the future. Expectations can shift demand and supply curves as easily as actual demand and supply shocks. The problem he said was that economists had no great insights into the formation of expectations. Three Senators chuckled when Alex said they should invite a psychologist to the next hearing.

Alex concluded his remarks by saying that the Department of Energy did not expect long lasting volatility before markets returned to relative stability. He said DOE would continue to monitor the situation but that no immediate policy changes were in order.

Joe Throckmorton was next, and he was a very good speaker. He began by explaining a little about his business and its more than 40 year history. He told them that many independent operators, such as himself, had made and lost fortunes in the oil and gas industry. He said the difficulty of running a business like his was that each investment in leases and drilling was a gamble on the future price of oil or gas – not today's price. We don't drill dry holes anymore; the gamble is all on price. He then told a story about Boone Pickens. In early July 2008, West Texas Intermediate briefly hit $147 per barrel. Boone was interviewed on TV that week and said crude would be selling for $200 per barrel by December. Boone was a little bit off in his forecast. By December, crude was $40 per barrel. Boone, Throckmorton continued, knew as much about the industry as anyone. Go figure.

Then Throckmorton said something quite remarkable: "I am honored to be here, and I am more than willing to help you out in any way that I can, but I am a little perplexed as to why you are holding this meeting. There is not much you can do about oil and gas price volatility. A very knowledgeable forecaster once told me not to look at oil prices every day, it will just drive you crazy. I offer you the same advice."

The senator from New Jersey left the room. From the expression on his face, it was easy to tell that he was not hearing what he wanted to hear. A junior staffer came into the room and whispered something to Brinkman, who promptly joined the senator from New Jersey on the way out the door. Hinton's testimony was next. He had a lot to say.

His first topic was the supply of oil and gas. Hinton told the committee that the current volatility had nothing to do with the supply of oil and gas. Nothing much had happened in the last few days to change supply. The U.S. and the world are not running out of oil. For more than a century we have been told that the supply of oil is finite and that we will use it all up before long. That is why Teddy Roosevelt created the Naval Petroleum reserve in Elks Hills, California and why we created the

179

Strategic Petroleum Reserve (SPR) in the 1970s. Releasing oil from the SPR would not stop the volatility in oil prices. The SPR involves pumping oil from deep in the ground and then pumping it into another hole deep in the ground. It makes little sense. The cheapest place to store oil is where it is.

As for the long run, Hinton said that as little as a decade ago, the phrase peak oil meant peak oil supply. Today, peak oil refers to peak oil demand. The world is floating in oil. So-called reserves do not refer to how much oil is in the ground. Reserves refer to what producers estimate as the amount of oil they can extract given today's prices and technology. In the last decade the U.S. and the World have produced more oil than was in 'proven reserves' ten years ago and reserves have only increased. It is not that anyone is trying to be deceptive about reserves, it is that both technology and prices change all the time and so do reserves.

Hinton's next topic was the demand for oil and gas. He told the committee that the world consumes about 100 million barrels of oil per day, with the U.S. accounting for about 20 million barrels per day. Neither U.S. nor world demand is going to change this year or next very much. We could be at or near the peak consumption of oil, but not natural gas. Transportation is a major component of oil demand. The reason this demand may have peaked is twofold: increases in the efficiency of internal combustion engines and growing sales of electric vehicles. The sales of electric vehicles will continue to grow, and all major manufacturers have committed to electrifying their offerings either partially or completely. But that is a medium to long term issue and has little to do with today's volatility.

Hinton explained that the current volatility was fairly easy to explain. Oil prices are determined at the margin, that is the last barrel produced. A two or three percent change in supply or demand may not seem like much, but it is if you are left holding oil that no one wants or can't get oil that everyone wants. This means that oil prices depend on other things besides underlying supply and demand factors.

Geopolitical instability and rumors of what may or may not happen in world markets can change oil prices one way or the other very suddenly. In the 1990s, it was literally true that a couple of kidnappings in Nigeria could cause the price of oil to jump by ten dollars a barrel. That is no longer the case but rumors that China may increase its imports or that the Saudis may cut production can send oil markets into a tizzy. Financial speculators, who risk billions of dollars in the futures market, react and over-react to such rumors and events quickly. No one wants to lock in a six-month futures contract on oil at $100 per barrel, when they have no idea what the actual price in six months might be.

Hinton then talked about policy. He told the committee that policy options were limited because the current volatility was in both directions. Releasing oil from the SPR, he said had already been discussed and rejected by his colleagues on the panel. Price controls were unlikely to be effective. Would you impose a price ceiling or a price floor on oil markets? Could you do both and at what price? You certainly don't want to disrupt production with price controls. The oil companies could be nationalized, as many nations have done this, but how would that stop the volatility? The one thing that might work is for the U.S. government to directly enter the oil markets, buying and selling on both the spot and futures markets. A few billion dollars would be enough to have an impact on the markets, but government traders would need to have a strategy that could outsmart the markets. Hinton did not recommend that. It might not even be possible.

The chair of the committee, Senator Wilson, began the questioning.

He asked the panel how to implement policies that would accelerate the energy transition and get us out of this mess with fossil fuels once and for all.

Alex Greenwood, the DOE economist, replied that his agency had promoted the use of wind, solar, and nuclear power for many years under both Democratic and Republican administrations, but speeding up the energy transition would be a difficult task accompanied by many failures.

Senator Wilson was not satisfied with Greenwood's answer and remarked that DOE had also promoted the use of fossil fuels. Senator Wilson had barely finished his comment when Brinkman appeared again and whispered something in his ear. Senator Wilson announced, "We have something of a crisis. Mr. Brinkman will summarize the situation."

Brinkman reported, "The Russians have closed Nordstream 1, which supplies natural gas to Europe. If this is not bad enough, there have been two explosions at the Henry Hub in Louisiana, disrupting natural gas supplies for much of the nation. Two major refineries – one in California and one in New Jersey are offline but the causes are unknown. In addition, the entire electrical grid in Pakistan has shut down. Prices of oil and natural gas have skyrocketed, the Dow Jones Index is down nearly 1,000 points and it seems to be falling more even as we talk."

Senator Wilson said that before he concluded the meeting he would like to hear from the panel. He added that he thought the president should speak to the nation on the crisis this evening.

Alex Goodman said that he was confident that DOE was actively monitoring the situation and would report to Senator Wilson and the president as soon as possible.

Joe Throckmorton advised the committee not to panic. He added that he thought the president should wait to address the nation until more of the facts are known. Speaking now would just add to the widespread feeling of panic.

Hinton was also blunt and to the point: "I agree with my colleagues on the panel. The president should wait to address the nation. The market reaction to these events is not justified. The day traders and computer algorithms are to blame. I don't give financial advice, but this does not look like a buying opportunity to me. Looking at the events one at a time, there is no reason for anyone to panic. The Pakistani electrical grid goes down frequently. It is a bit unusual that it is the entire grid. The Russians have shut down Nordstream 1 for maintenance several times in the past and this may be one of those times. Mr. Brinkman indicated that the Russians have not stated a reason for the shutdown. We don't yet know why the two refineries shut down. The refineries are large ones that consume nearly a million and a half barrels of oil per day. If they remain shut for more than a day or two, that will put downward pressure on WTI oil prices. The explosions at Henry Hub are concerning, but I am confident that the pipelines can be restored to service in weeks. It really is far too early to panic."

Senator Wilson thanked the panel and called an end to the hearing. Despite the apparent urgency of the situation, Brinkman took a few minutes to talk with each member of the panel. He told them that he had been pleased with the panel's testimony and that given the current problems he wanted all of them to be available for further analysis and testimony on short notice. In turn, each panel member assured Brinkman that they were available for anything he might need.

Joe Throckmorton then asked Hinton if they could have a private conversation. "Of course." Hinton answered. Throckmorton then said he wanted to hire Hinton as his chief economist.

Hinton asked, "What is the chief in this title. You don't have any other economists." Throckmorton laughed and told him that what he really wanted to do was to groom Hinton to be the next CEO of his company. He explained that his two kids wanted nothing to do with running the company. He said, I listened to your testimony today and in the past. You know the industry and you have a lot of common sense. I have done a background check on you. No doubt in my mind, you are the one I want. I will pay you double what you are getting at the university. I will put enough money in an escrow account that is yours if it doesn't work out. You will have the resources you need, and I don't care where you live. What I want to do is to buy a condo on South Padre Island and watch the sun come up and go down knowing that I have someone competent to run the company. I'll give you a week to decide." Hinton said he would consider the offer seriously.

Hinton walked out of the building and called Deuce. Previously, they had agreed to meet the next day, but Deuce said they should meet this afternoon if that was possible. Hinton said, "Absolutely." Oddly, Deuce said he wanted to meet off-campus, meaning somewhere other than Langley. They agreed to meet at the Lincoln Memorial in an hour. Deuce did not know that this was one of Hinton's favorite places. From there, they could walk and talk without being interrupted or overheard. Hinton dropped his file folder, which contained only an unused yellow pad, in the trash and walked to the Lincoln Memorial. He had always been stunned by the beauty and majesty of the mall and the buildings surrounding it. More importantly if he took his time the trip would be just about an hour.

Deuce smiled when he arrived and saw that Hinton was already there. His greeting was, "Turn your cell phone off and take the SIMM card out of it. That way we can talk without being listened to."

Hinton did as he was told and then Deuce said,

"Hell of a mess we've got here. In truth we have more than one mess and I need your help. The Director is on-board, and we are the only three people in the loop. Let's talk about the public crisis first. Do you know anything that hasn't been reported yet?"

"I talked to an old friend who is the operations manager at one of the refineries. The problem is that they had performed a software update last night. As sometimes happens, the new software contained a flaw that shut down both refineries. The software had signaled that there was too much pressure in parts of the system and that this presented a safety issue. There was no choice but to shut them down. The software engineers are attempting to restore the older version, but this will take some time. It is a lot more complicated than an update to the operating system on your computer. The best guess is that both refineries should be operational by tomorrow morning. The good news is that there is no evidence that the computer systems were hacked. The bad news is that most of the refineries in North America use the same software. The other refineries have been notified that they should not install the new software, but who knows if that message was on time. CNN and the other news networks will have this story within the hour but for now, we are among the very few who know this."

Deuce nodded and said,

"That's better than I thought it would be. It reminds me of the airline scheduling software glitches that threw the whole system into chaos with thousands of flights canceled and delayed for days. One of these days we will wake up and none of it will work. Transportation systems, pipeline systems, banking, finance. You name it and it will all go down. But tell me about Henry Hub. And I need to confess I am only vaguely aware of what that is."

185

Hinton said, "Don't be embarrassed. Most people outside of the industry don't know what Henry Hub is. In Erath, Louisiana, a small town just south of Lafayette, several natural gas pipelines meet in one place. This includes nine interstate pipelines and another three or four intra-state pipelines. It is the largest natural gas shipping point in the world. In addition to pipelines there are processing and pressurization facilities at the Hub. And the price paid for Henry Hub gas is the benchmark price used throughout the nation for natural gas. The benchmark price for LNG, including exports, is also in reference to Henry Hub. So, think of Henry Hub as a transportation and pricing center for natural gas. The prices, of course, are not determined at the Hub. They are determined in commodities markets. We don't yet know the extent of damage at Henry Hub or what caused the explosions."

"Thanks. I suppose that there are people at the Agency that know all of that, but I am not one of them. I do understand the importance of Nordstream but we will just need to wait and see what the Russians have to say about it. We need to talk about our other issue."

Hinton hesitated. "Before we start, here is a summary of my expenses. I still have about five thousand dollars left and I will be glad to give it to you. Unfortunately, I don't have receipts for a lot of this. I hope that is okay."

"Thank you for the summary. I don't care about the receipts and for now, I want you to keep the balance. I will explain later. "The DC police, the FBI, and the Agency are convinced that Ross killed Patti Walker. After a lot of effort, we have located three additional murders with similar characteristics. The victims were all female, and all were tied up in a fashion similar to Patti. The first murder we uncovered was just outside Chiang Mai, Thailand near one of the many temples that the city is famous for. This murder was almost identical to Patti Walker's murder. Chiang Mai is a popular resort area, and the Thai authorities were reluctant to have the murder reported in the press. They also withheld the event from the international data bases. We are trying to find out if Ross was in Thailand at the time."

Hinton interjected, "I don't know the exact timing but a couple of years ago Ross visited Taiwan, Singapore, and Thailand. I can probably find out the dates from his department."

Deuce stopped walking and looked at Hinton before continuing. "That would be useful. The second similar murder occurred in Parral, Mexico which is about 150 miles south of Chihuahua City. The similarities are too difficult to ignore. The young woman was tied up just like Patti. The wounds were also similar. The Mexican authorities deal with so many murders that they assumed this was cartel activity and did not spend a lot of time investigating it. We know that Ross attended a conference in Chihuahua City at the time of this murder."

Hinton told Deuce that he had been at the same conference and that Ross had taken a side-trip after the conference to Parral. He wanted to see the place where Pancho Villa lived and died after the revolution.

Deuce continued, "The third murder was closer to home. A young woman was found murdered in Wilburton, Oklahoma. All the signs suggest it was done by the same person who killed Patti."

Hinton told Deuce that Wilburton was the closest city to Robbers Cave State Park, a favorite getaway for several faculty members he knew including Ross. The park has nice cabins built in the 1930s and it is a very peaceful spot.

Deuce went on with his story. "We are searching for additional incidents, and I think we will find them. The DC prosecutor's office told the police and the FBI that coincidence is not enough to arrest Ross, much less convict him. They need forensic evidence, DNA, fingerprints,

187

or something that proves Ross was there. We are looking but so far, we have come up empty. I know that you think Ross is incapable of committing crimes like this, but the circumstantial evidence is powerful."

Hinton blurted out, "Can I change my mind about Ross? I am convinced that you are on to something. Still, with no forensic evidence, everyone should keep an open mind about Ross. Remember, innocent until proven guilty."

Deuce agreed and said, "But there is more. There is good reason to believe that Ross is working for the Russians. Remember what I told you earlier about Dimitri Nogolov and the large bank deposits just before and after Patti's murder."

Hinton still wondered whether Ross could really be that stupid. The Russia connection to Ross did not surprise Hinton since he had heard it before. The next thing Deuce told him was a shock to his system.

"I no longer trust Johnston, who has been acting strangely over the last few weeks. His weekly reports are inconsistent and seem to be incomplete. His conversations are vague. He seems to be hiding something, but I don't know what it is. The last time he called, I recorded the conversation and took it to our voice analysts. Independently, they both said that Johnston seemed stressed and deceptive. The second one went further and said he was lying. These guys almost always get it right. The firm that Johnston worked for in Texas once had a contract with London Energy Consultants. While doing that work, Johnston met several high-level managerial types in Gazprom. He reported that when we hired him. We encouraged him to keep those contacts alive. I don't know exactly what to think, but you should not trust him to tell you the truth. I don't think he poses a physical threat to you but be careful. If you are wondering why I am telling you this stuff, it is because we still need you involved in this case, and we need you to brief us on the volatility crisis. That is also why I told you to keep the expense money. Spend it on anything you think is necessary."

"Deuce, I don't work for you anymore. I don't want to work for the Agency. Doing so would ruin my academic career if it ever became public. As for the current market crisis, my analysis is always public and you or anyone else can find out what I have to say."

After some discussion about the boundaries Hinton imposed on their relationship, the two men agreed to stay in touch. Hinton knew exactly what he needed to do next.

Chapter 16

Home Again

Even with Millie's expertise with airline tickets, the only available flight from DC to Oklahoma City the next day involved a first-class seat. Hinton did not mind the extra expense and he understood that this ticket was likely to be from his own pocket. If he was filthy rich, flying first-class or on a Learjet would always be his choice. That thought made him think of Joe Throckmorton's offer. If he accepted it, he could always fly first-class and stay at expensive hotels. He quickly dismissed the idea. He would think about that offer later. Now he was just arriving at National Airport on the Metro. He had always liked National better than Dulles, especially before National had been remodeled and renamed. Unlike the cookie cutter modern airports, at one time the place had character.

Hinton had already checked in at his gate when Lloyd Brinkman called. Aggravated by the call, Hinton answered it anyway. Brinkman told him that Senator Wilson wanted to talk to him again. The Senator had been intrigued by Hinton's suggestion of direct government purchases of oil to stabilize the markets. Hinton explained that he was only minutes away from boarding a flight. They agreed on a video conference call for 8 am the next day. Brinkman apologized for how early (7 am) that would be in Oklahoma. Hinton said he did not care. He was an early riser.

Hinton's itinerary took him from DC to Dallas, where he would change planes for the short flight to Oklahoma City. The flight was smooth and on-time. In first-class Hinton had plenty of leg room and shortly after take-off he fell asleep. That was a good thing. He had not been sleeping well and badly needed the rest. He woke up as the plane was landing in Dallas and the flight attendant came by to check that his seatbelt was fastened. He was surprised that he had not thought about any of the things he was concerned about. Ross, Johnston, the mystery woman, U.S. Senators, Millie, Linda, and the job offer never crossed his mind.

Hinton arrived in Oklahoma City on-time and in good spirits. He had only carry-ons for baggage and went directly to the parking lot to pick up his Jeep. He went directly home to his house in Norman and when he arrived, Fergie went wild and for a while would not leave him alone. He felt honored that someone had missed him. In a few minutes, Millie and Tanya arrived. He had not expected to see both. They explained that they were there to check on Fergie, not him. Most of the time Hinton had been gone, Tanya slept at the house because Fergie seemed to be lonely. Tanya, not Millie, mentioned the broken washing machine and Hinton's promise to fix it. On the way out the door, Millie said that President Henderson wanted to see him as soon as possible. Usually, that meant an 8 am meeting. Without explanation, Hinton said 8:30 would be better.

Hinton was ready for the early morning video call from Senator Wilson. Well before 6 am he was up, dressed, and had finished a light breakfast. He had brewed a pot of coffee and placed it within reach of his computer. The call came in at exactly 7 am. Brinkman was on the line with the senator. With not so much as a good morning, the Senator began the conversation.

"I am intrigued by your idea that the federal government could buy

192

and sell oil and gas to stabilize prices, but I have several questions. First, how much would it cost."

"Let's start with oil. That is the easier market to deal with. Oil markets are world markets and as you know, the world consumes 100 million barrels of oil per day. On the supply side of the equation one or two million barrels a day is enough to have a major impact on markets. When the Saudis or OPEC or Russia announce a change in production of a million barrels, the markets often go crazy. We have seen that time and again. A million barrels of oil at $100 per barrel is $100 million a day. At most, you would need double that to move the markets. Intervening on that scale for a single day would not do the trick. A one-time purchase or sale of a million barrels would hardly be noticed. What would be needed is the ability to buy and sell over a prolonged period, perhaps many weeks or a few months. So, let's call that a billion dollars a week. My guess is that a fund of $50 or $60 billion would be needed because you must have the flexibility to go big if you need to."

"In the grand scheme of things, that is not a lot of money to stabilize energy markets, and I might add, financial markets. I still have a lot of questions. Surely, it can't be that simple, or is it?"

"What I told you about costs is the macro view of things. The details are really complicated. For example, there is no such thing as THE price of oil. Look on any of the industry apps and you can find 150 to 200 oil prices. Not all oil is alike. It varies in quality from light sweet crude from West Texas to heavy sour crude from Canadian oil sands, for example. Light refers to viscosity—how easily it flows. Sweet and sour refer to sulfur content. It makes a difference. Then, there is location. Oil needs to be in the right place at the right time and transporting it is not cheap."

"What else might complicate this?"

"Two things will make it difficult, but not impossible. Oil is sold on both the spot market and the futures market. Buyers and sellers need to be very sophisticated about what it is they are buying or selling and that would be true of any government agency trying to buy and sell enough to influence prices. Contango and backwardation are things to think about. Contango occurs when the futures price is higher than the spot price. Backwardation occurs when the futures price is lower than the spot price. Something else to think about is what we are trying to accomplish. Reasonably stable prices is one goal, but at what level of prices. Oil companies would obviously prefer high and stable prices. Consumers would prefer low and stable prices. There will be some hard choices to make."

"That all sounds like technical issues to me. I would worry that voters would rant about government interference in free markets. They would all tell me that this is unprecedented. What the hell do we tell them?"

"It is not unprecedented. The federal government has been 'interfering' with agricultural markets for more than a century. We have given them price supports and often pay them not to grow a particular crop. Those farmers and some large corporations cash their government checks, publicly proclaim the virtues of the market, and vote for candidates who don't support these subsidies. Consumers and producers would probably make some noise, but they would be careful not to make too much noise."

"Has this ever been done in energy markets?"

"Absolutely and it is still going on. In the early 1990s when the Soviet Union was collapsing the US purchased a lot of high energy uranium (HEU) rather than let it fall into the hands of terrorists. Your former colleague Pete Domenici led the effort in the Senate to make the purchase. He was hardly a bleeding-heart liberal, but he thought this was necessary for national security. Ever since then, whenever the price of uranium increases, DOE, which holds the uranium, releases more on the market. You can only imagine what the uranium mining companies say about this policy. It is only one example of government intervention in energy markets. When it will end, no one knows. DOE refuses to tell anyone how large their stock of uranium is. There is a name for it. In the industry, it is known as FSU or Former Soviet Union."

"Okay, so it has been done before. This would probably take a congressional appropriation of funds for the $50 billion or so to intervene in oil markets. That will be hard to pull off with people on both sides of the aisle promising to reduce government spending. Any ideas?"

"Yes. The Federal Reserve, especially the Federal Reserve Bank of New York, intervenes in foreign exchange markets all the time. They do so without publicity or pushback from anyone. They do it without congressional appropriations or permission. Right now, they have about nine trillion dollars on their balance sheet consisting mainly of Government bonds and mortgage backed securities acquired during the Great Recession. If Chairman Powell and his friends could be convinced, expanding the FED balance sheet by another $50 billion to stabilize oil markets would hardly be noticed."

"Powell is a hard nut to crack. That might be possible but are there other ways to do it?"

"Yes. In 1993 the Mexican economy was on the verge of collapse. The peso was falling rapidly, inflation was high, and it looked again like Mexico was going to default on its debt, most of which was owned by US banks. The debt was accumulated during the peak of Mexican oil production when the need for capital expenditures was great. When oil prices collapsed, Mexico was in serious trouble. It was a terrible situation. Congressional leaders told the Clinton administration that there would be no more bailout money for Mexico but behind the scenes they told President Clinton that if he could raise the money elsewhere, they would not object. The Clinton Administration showed remarkable ingenuity. In a matter of days, they put together a $40 billion aid package for Mexico with no Congressional appropriation. They used some money from an obscure federal fund called the Economic Stabilization Fund. They got additional funds from the International Monetary Fund and the Bank for International Settlements. The crisis was averted. No one objected. A similar procedure could be used again."

"What are the risks?"

"The most obvious risk is buying or selling the wrong amount of oil. It would be possible to make an even bigger mess. Trading just the right amount is a tricky business. The other kind of risk is the reaction of the Saudis and Russians. They too are major producers, and they are not passive actors in this game."

"If you were in charge, what would you do?"

"I would wait a few weeks and see if the markets don't settle down on their own and at the same time prepare to implement an intervention plan. "

"I am going to float your idea with some of my colleagues and I am going to bring it up tomorrow when I meet with the President. You don't need to be concerned. I will claim this idea as my own."

Wilson thanked Hinton and then said something that caught Hinton off-guard.

"I think you should run for Senate. Senator Hammond is no longer capable of doing his job. I think you could win and from what I hear, so do a lot of other people in Oklahoma."

"Senator, I am honored by your suggestion, but I would not stand a chance. I am a native Texan and an academic. Neither of those things would go over well in Oklahoma."

"That's not what I am hearing from my sources. You have name recognition in the state and a lot of people who would be willing help."

"You are not from Oklahoma. Who do you hear all this stuff from?"

"I have known your boss, Jim Henderson for thirty-five years. We are close friends, and he is a very astute analyst of political issues."

The conversation ended with Hinton making a joke about politics. Brinkman, who had been on the call with Wilson never said a word. The conversation had taken longer than Hinton expected, and he needed to hurry to get to Henderson's office.

On the way into Henderson's office, Hinton spoke briefly to Millie. Henderson greeted him warmly, but Hinton took no comfort in the greeting. He knew that Henderson greeted everyone in all circumstances warmly. He would greet you warmly even if he was going to fire you.

"You are going to be a busy little boy this week."

"Maybe so but you need to remember that in the summertime I am not on your payroll."

Henderson laughed and continued, "On Thursday we are going to have a big to do with the Oil and Gas Association where you and Ross will be presented with endowed chairs. They will also announce the construction of a building devoted to the study of the oil and gas industry. It is a big deal. The governor will be there and so will you. If Ross doesn't show up, I have half a mind to fire him."

Hinton responded,

"I can do without the governor who will no doubt praise this great institution of higher learning even though he convinced the legislature to cut all higher ed funding just a few months ago. He is a two-faced SOB. As for Ross, I am not his keeper, but I think he will be here. I am not so sure he should be. His presence may cause you great embarrassment. The DC police, the FBI, and our other friends are convinced he killed Patti Walker. The circumstantial evidence is strong but there is as of now no forensic evidence, so they have held off on charging him."

"You are right about the governor. I hope you are wrong about Ross's imminent arrest. That would be very embarrassing. You also need to check in with Athletics. They really need you to take care of some things."

"I have already checked in with the AD and he is convening the appeals committee. I wish it were something other than that, but consider it done."

On the way out, he arranged to talk to Millie after work. He spent the rest of the afternoon taking care of various issues in the athletics department. He really liked the athletes and was uncomfortable that the committee had voted unanimously against the volleyball student. It was an unusual case. Volleyball students almost never get in trouble – academically or otherwise.

Early in the evening, Hinton went to Millie's house and repaired the washing machine, which took very little time, but probably saved Millie a hundred dollars or so. Millie seemed a little distraught and after thanking him for the repair job, she said,

"I have something to tell you that you are not going to like very much but you need to know what's going on with me. I have three job offers on the table and I am going to take one of them. I could become the first female city manager of Norman. I could be the executive director of the Oil and Gas Association. I could become the operations manager at Will Rogers Airport. The airport job involves the most stress and pays the most, and it would get me back to the airline industry. I will decide in the next week or so but in any case, I am leaving the university."

Hinton took the news in stride but said, "Millie, how can I possibly do my job without the fixer? This will be a terrible loss for the university community."

Millie was not finished delivering bad news. She continued, "I love my job and the university, but I can't stay. For more than a year, Jim Henderson and I have been in a serious relationship."

Hinton reacted before Millie could finish. "Damn it! Millie. You know the rules about employee relationships on campus better than I do. This could cost Henderson his job and yours too if you stay for any length of time. What the hell were you thinking?"

Millie looked downcast and paused before speaking. "We weren't thinking. It started innocently enough with a dinner or two and just evolved. When I took the job in the president's office, we both understood and agreed that it was for a few weeks at most. The office was really disorganized, and he needed some help to fix it. I will be long gone before our relationship becomes public. We are both adults and knew the risks we were taking, but it will work out just fine. I thought you might be upset because it would throw a monkey-wrench into any potential relationship between you and me. Jim understands our close friendship and that does not need to change."

Hinton smiled reassuringly and wrapped his arms around Millie before saying, "Don't worry about me. I am a big boy and I have been disappointed several times about relationships. Other than keeping my mouth shut, is there anything I can do to help you?"

Millie said to just keep being her friend. She was sure she would need that.

Hinton left Millie's house and walked the two blocks to his own home. He was disappointed, confused and a bit angry. Millie trusted him with everything including her daughter but did not trust him enough to reveal her relationship with Henderson earlier. About half-way home, he laughed. He had always liked Marty Robins' song "Don't worry 'bout me" and realized he had used that phrase with Millie. He wondered if Millie caught it. Sometime he would ask her. He wondered if Linda knew about Millie's relationship when she advised him to back off. He called Linda and invited her to dinner on Friday night. When she appeared reluctant, he said they could go to Vast, an excellent restaurant at the top of the Devon Tower.

On Thursday, the ceremony with the Oil and Gas Association went about as smoothly as you could expect. The governor was there and so was Ross. Of course, the governor spoke first, taking credit for everything good about the university including the success of the athletics programs. He praised Henderson whom he despised almost as much as Henderson despised him. Fortunately, he was in a hurry and turned the program back to Henderson who, as expected, praised the governor for his higher education initiatives. This false praise was not missed by the audience, some of whom chuckled, and one slightly embarrassed member of the audience laughed loud enough that everyone on stage could hear him.

The representatives from the Oil and Gas Association presented the checks for the endowed chairs to President Henderson and joked that he should cash them before the price of oil dropped even further. Then, they announced that they were also funding the construction of a new building for the study of the industry. It was an impressive gift of $25 million. They were careful to say that these gifts were not an infringement of academic freedom. There were no strings attached. Ross, Hinton, and whoever else might benefit from these gifts could do research on whatever they liked, could write whatever they liked, and carry their

200

messages to the public even if this meant being critical of oil and gas or fossil fuels more generally. Ross and Hinton were each given about thirty seconds to offer their thanks. Henderson seemed relieved when it was all over, and the audience applauded appropriately. Life could go back to normal, whatever that meant.

Hinton wanted to clear his desk of the many things he had neglected during his travels to Europe and then head to Big Bend for what he thought was some well-deserved time off. Millie's conversation with him the night before was still on his mind. In light of that, he did not bother to ask Millie if she wanted to go with him as they had done several times in the past. He did not really care what Ross was up to, he just hoped that Ross was not arrested before he went to Big Bend.

The Friday night dinner with Linda was the most fun he had experienced in a long time. The Devon Tower is the tallest building in Oklahoma City. The views were magnificent, and the meal was superb. The desserts were downright sinful. The service was outstanding. The two bottles of French chardonnay they shared put them in a very relaxed mood. Linda claimed she was unaware of any new relationship in Millie's life. Hinton did not tell her who this new love was. They had walked the mile to Devon Tower. Parking was always a nuisance. When the meal was finally finished, they called an Uber for the ride back to Linda's condo. Hinton had consumed most of the wine and quickly fell asleep on Linda's couch. He did not wake up until early the next morning.

Late Saturday morning Hinton was taking Fergie for a walk or maybe it was Fergie taking him for a walk when his cell phone rang. With no preliminaries Millie said,

"You need to get over here now. Ross is dead and the president needs to talk to you now. Where are you?"

"I am walking with Fergie on the east side of campus near the old university golf course."

"Bring Fergie and get to the president's office as quickly as you can. This could be a bigger mess than anything we have seen on campus since they fired Barry Switzer."

When he arrived at Henderson's office, the president did not seem to notice Fergie who sat quietly by the chair Hinton had been offered. Henderson said nothing for a minute or two and so Hinton broke the silence.

"How did Ross die? Was his death from natural causes like a heart attack or did someone kill him?"

"Ross was murdered sometime last night. The Norman City Police and the Oklahoma State Bureau of Investigation (OSBI) are still trying to figure out what happened. Apparently, Ross died from a single gunshot wound to the head. The medical examiner is conducting an autopsy as we speak. So far, there are no suspects. OSBI has asked the FBI to give them a profile of the likely killer, but you know what that will look like – white male, age 25 to 45, highly educated, and probably known to the victim."

"Who found him? The body could have stayed there for days before anyone missed Ross."

"Ross was supposed to play golf with three others early this morning – a 7 AM tee time, I think. Ross did not show up. He is known to be late for a lot of things but never late for a hard-to-get tee time. One of his fellow golfers decided to go check on him. His car was there but the golfer got no response and called the police. I don't know much more than that."

"I'll be damned. There have been times when I could have killed him myself and I am sure you have felt the same way on occasion."

"Don't even joke about that. I am sure the Norman PD or OSBI will want to interview anyone who knew him or had seen him in the last few days. That includes me. You knew him better than I did. Do you have any idea who might have done this?"

"No, but from what you have told me this looks like the work of a professional. Most amateurs can't kill someone with a single shot."

"That was my thought exactly, but other than watching crime shows on TV I don't have any experience with this sort of thing. I am going to need your help dealing with several things. What a mess and it would have to happen the day after the ceremony with the governor and the Oil and Gas folks. I would like you to stick around for a while."

"No problem. Just let me know what you need."

Millie entered Henderson's office and interrupted the conversation. She said she had just talked to the Norman PD detective in charge of the case. She gave a thorough summary of her conversation,

"The medical examiner confirmed that Ross died from a single gunshot wound to the head. The detective said he should not tell me the rest but that it would be public soon enough. The weapon appears to have been a small caliber pistol – maybe a 22. There is no exit wound, and no bullet was recovered. The bullet disintegrated into dozens if not hundreds of pieces as soon as it entered his head. Bullets like that are not for sale at the local sporting goods store. Chances are that the shooter made the bullet himself. There will be no ballistic evidence that amounts to anything. No lands and grooves to identify the weapon. The detective wants to talk to all three of us as soon as he can. "

Hinton told Henderson and Millie that he would take Fergie back to the house and return within thirty minutes. Fergie was well-behaved but Hinton did not want the dog to be there when the police showed up. For some reason, Fergie never reacted well to people in uniforms.

When Hinton returned, Detective Joe McDonald from the Norman PD had just arrived. McDonald had grown up in Chicago and spent more than two decades with the Chicago police department. He was an experienced homicide detective who had dealt with more than a hundred homicides. He retired from the Chicago PD as soon as he could and then took a job as Chief of Detectives in the Norman PD. He knew how to conduct an interview.

The interviews took place individually, as they should. Henderson's interview was short and to the point. McDonald asked about his relationship with Ross and Henderson explained that their relationship was strictly professional. He had never socialized with Ross. McDonald asked about Henderson's activities on Friday night and was told that he had been at a university event until about 10 pm. There were about fifty people present who could vouch for the president's location. McDonald thanked Henderson and explained that he was not a person of interest in the case, but that the question about Friday night had to be asked.

Millie's interview was next, and McDonald asked the same questions. Millie also explained that her contacts with Ross were strictly professional. She did not know him well. Millie had also been at the university event with Henderson and fifty others.

McDonald's interview with Hinton took more time. Hinton explained that he had known Ross since they were in graduate school many years ago and that he had been instrumental in getting Ross his job at OU. Hinton also said that despite their long association, they were not close friends and rarely saw each other off campus. When asked about an alibi for Friday evening, Hinton laughed and said he had dinner with his ex-wife in Oklahoma City and then fell asleep on her couch. He gave Linda's phone number to McDonald who commented that his ex-wife would have nothing to do with him – much less have dinner with him.

McDonald said that as a matter of thoroughness he needed to check with Linda.

When all of them were together again after the interviews were completed, McDonald said,

"Thank you for your cooperation. I mean it. You might be surprised how often people won't discuss anything with the police. Unlike in Chicago, most murders in Norman, there are not many, involve a family member or close friend. That does not seem to be the case with this one. This looks more like a professional hit job. The three of you are not suspects or persons of interest, but as a police officer, I must keep an open mind. I will keep President Henderson informed of what we find out."

Hinton agreed to postpone his trip to Big Bend for a few days. Henderson asked him if Ross had any close relatives and indicated that his personnel record said to notify Hinton in case of emergency. Hinton laughed and then more seriously told Henderson that Ross's father was dead but that he thought his mother still lived in the family home near Midland. Hinton thought Ross had a sister living somewhere in Dallas, but he had never met her and had no contact information.

As soon as he left Henderson's office, he called Linda to give her a heads-up that the police would be contacting her about where he was on Friday night. Linda had not yet heard of the murder, but she remarked that she had never liked the man.

Hinton's next call, actually three calls, an hour apart, was to Johnston, who did not answer his phone. Someone at the Agency needed to know what was going on so Hinton reluctantly called Deuce, who was unaware of the murder but did have other information. Deuce said that the FBI had uncovered two additional murders similar to Patti Walker's. One was in Questa, New Mexico, a small mining town near the ski resort of Taos. The other case was in Redstone Colorado, an even smaller mining community south of Carbondale. The two cases were three and four years old and had not attracted widespread attention. There were no suspects in either case. Deuce did not know why Johnston did not answer his phone but said that he was certain Johnston would call back at some point.

Hinton spent the rest of the weekend taking Fergie on long walks and doing chores around the house. Fergie seemed to enjoy the walks and the dog was a wonderful companion but no help at all in figuring out whether Ross was connected to several murders or who killed Ross.

By Monday morning Hinton had concluded that Ross's murder and the others might remain unsolved. Some questions just can't be answered. He remembered vividly when he had learned that some questions might not have an answer. As an undergraduate, he had read Hemingway's "Snows of Kilimanjaro." In the first paragraph, Hemingway described the carcass of a lion at 14,000 feet on the mountain. Hemingway explained that lions don't belong at 14,000 feet. They don't live there, and they don't hunt there. Then, Hemingway posed the unanswerable question by saying "Find out what that lion was doing on the side of the mountain, and you will have figured out the secret of the universe." Any reader, including a then 19-year-old Hinton, understood immediately that no answer was possible. After reading Hemingway, Hinton was always comfortable with the idea that there were questions with no answers. That realization was an important part of his intellectual development.

Hinton's thoughts were interrupted when Millie called and said that Henderson wanted to see him early in the afternoon. She asked if 1 PM would work and Hinton told her he would arrive shortly before 1 PM. As he approached the Administration Building, Hinton reminded himself of his own rules. Institutional loyalty is a one-way street. You can be loyal to the institution, but the institution doesn't give a damn about you. Never trust an administrator, not because they are all bad people but because they have very different goals than any faculty member. Finally, don't be a fool. If a university president asks you to do something, do it, no matter how outrageous or ill-advised the request might be.

Henderson opened the conversation by telling Hinton that the police were no closer to solving Ross's murder. They still had no DNA evidence, no fingerprints, no weapon, and no witnesses. Then, he continued,

"We need to put this thing behind us as soon as possible. We are going to hold a celebration of life ceremony for Ross on Friday in the student union auditorium. Millie spent most of the morning calling churches to see if Ross was a member of any of them. None of them said they knew Ross although two churches volunteered to hold a service for Ross. After consulting with various deans, I concluded that it must be held on campus."

Hinton said something like "Good decision" and Henderson continued,

"As you probably know, by long-standing tradition the university president does not speak at such events. We have thousands of employees, retirees, students, and former students. If the president spoke at one funeral, the pressure to speak at others would be unbearable. No one in the history department thinks they knew Ross well enough to speak. You knew him longer than anyone on campus. Will you do it?"

Hinton, who made a habit of never attending funerals or so-called celebrations of life, reluctantly agreed to speak. Then Henderson made another request,

"We have 23 students registered for Ross's history of oil and gas class in the fall. No doubt it will fill up to the maximum of forty. That is a lot for an upper division history elective class. Will you teach the class?"

This one was easier for Hinton to agree to though teaching an extra class is a lot of work.

Hinton had no trouble filling the next three days with reasonably productive activity. Rather than being bored, he was busier than he wanted to be. He went to campus each morning. He revised the syllabus for the history of oil and gas industry class to his own liking. He completed a manuscript review for an academic journal that would soon be overdue. He talked to several coaches including the new head football coach about the upcoming season. He talked to some students even though there were very few of them around in the middle of the summer. Each day, he checked in with either Detective McDonald or Henderson seeking news on the case. There was no news and no new evidence. He also called Johnston every day but never connected and never received a call back.

On Friday, Hinton arrived at the auditorium a few minutes early and was told to take a seat on stage with the chair of the history department who would introduce him. Just before ten, a small crowd had gathered. Hinton's quick count was that there were about fifty people in the audience, most of whom were vice-presidents, deans, associate deans, and department heads. No doubt the president's office had something to do with their attendance. There were four or five faculty members from the history department and a few students. Ross's sister, who had been introduced to Hinton was also there, but not his mother. Detective McDonald was also in the audience toward the back of the auditorium. Hinton thought this was a very sad commentary on a man's life.

Just before being introduced, he spotted a familiar face in the audience. The mystery woman was seated in the middle of the auditorium. Hinton immediately wondered if she was the killer. There was absolutely nothing he could do about it. What could he do? Yelling out to Detective McDonald to arrest the woman was not an option. He had absolutely no evidence against her, just suspicions.

Hinton gave the eulogy, speaking mainly in generalities about what a great loss this was for the university community. The crowd did not seem to mind that his remarks did not last long. When asked, no one in the crowd volunteered to speak. The audience left quickly. The chair of the history department, a couple of deans and Henderson thanked him. The mystery woman disappeared without giving Hinton a chance to confront her. Hinton was glad it was over, looked forward to leaving town for his trip to Big Bend, and headed home to Fergie who was happy to see him.

Chapter 17

Big Bend

Hinton needed the peace and quiet of Big Bend and on Saturday morning he began packing his Jeep. His plan was to leave Fergie with Tanya. Fergie had other ideas and probably understood what packing the Jeep meant. Fergie stared at Hinton with a look that said: "You can't possibly leave me behind." As soon as possible Fergie had parked herself in the passenger seat. Hinton called Tanya and told her he would take Fergie with him.

Packing did not take much time for Hinton, and they were on the road in just a few minutes. Fergie was relaxed and seemed very pleased to be in the jeep. Hinton's thoughts turned to Big Bend. When anyone asked Hinton why he liked Big Bend so much he always gave the same answer: "The Big Bend is a thousand square miles without a McDonalds or a Starbucks." This was a simple way of describing something much more complex to people who probably did not want to hear a longer version. The vastness of the place is humbling. You could not look at it or view the stars at night without realizing that you are a tiny insignificant piece of the universe. The night skies in Big Bend look different than they do in more populated areas. People come from all over the world to look at the stars from an area with almost total darkness at night.

Hinton knew little about astronomy, but the night skies were impressive. More impressive to Hinton was that you could travel from cactus and creosote bushes to mountains and pine forests in just a few minutes. And there was the wildlife. Where else were you likely to encounter mountain lions, coyotes, javelina, wild burros, rattlesnakes, and porcupines in the wild. In the last decade or two, the Mexican Black Bear had returned after not being sighted in the Big Bend for more than half a century. Now they were everywhere. These creatures had not been hunted in seventy-five years and were generally unafraid of humans. The wildlife was not the reason that one or two visitors died in the park each year. Rather, people died in the park from stupidity. More than likely, they would die from heat and dehydration having taken a hike alone without water or any knowledge of what they were doing. The park rangers tried but could not wipe out stupidity.

Hinton recognized that all of that was true, but for him there was another, more basic reason that he loved the area. Big Bend felt like home, a place where nothing bad had ever happened to him. It was just a magical place.

Hinton took Highway 9 out of Norman and then got on the H. E. Bailey Turnpike which would take them to Lawton, about 90 miles away. From there, it was straight south to Wichita Falls and beyond. Just before the second Lawton exit, Hinton's cell phone rang. Hinton was tempted to ignore it, but he saw that the call was from Lloyd Brinkman. Hinton's phone was in a holder attached to the dash and he hit the answer button and told Brinkman he was driving and would call him back in a few minutes.

Hinton pulled off the highway and parked in a grocery store parking lot on Gore Boulevard, one of the main streets in Lawton. As promised, he called Brinkman back and Brinkman said,

"I just sent you two papers from the White House. One is a two-page executive summary, and the other is a bit longer. These have been circulating in the White House for several days. They are not classified but they are also not public –at least not yet. Senator Wilson wants to know what you think of them."

Hinton quickly read the two-page summary and responded to Brinkman,

"The two-pager looks exactly like what I told the Senator about intervening in oil and gas markets. Who wrote these?"

"Somebody on the Council of Economic Advisors wrote them. I think the two-pager was given to the President. No action has been taken yet. If you were talking to the president, what would you tell him?"

Hinton did not hesitate,

"I would advise the president to get everything in place, but not to execute the plan yet. The markets, including oil and gas, have calmed down a bit. There is no point in screwing things up if you don't need to. As I told the Senator before, the chances of making a mistake are high."

Brinkman told Hinton that he would pass that along to Senator Wilson and then asked if Hinton would be available for another conference call. Hinton told Brinkman that he had a tablet with him but that there might be times in the next few days when cell phone service was not available.

Hinton and Fergie got back on the highway and headed south toward Wichita Falls, sometimes known derogatorily as Whiskey Falls because it was a favorite drinking spot for the airmen at the base and the soldiers from Fort Sill in Lawton. They had barely crossed the Red River into Texas when Hinton's phone rang once again. This time it was Deuce. Hinton did not answer the call but pulled off the road at the first rest area in Texas. He called Deuce back, who without a greeting began the conversation,

"I have another problem. I still can't find Johnston. Have you seen him or heard from him? It would be no great loss if he disappeared, but he does work for me, and I feel obligated to find him."

"Deuce, I have not heard from him or seen him. I almost expected him to be at the ceremony for Ross, but he was a no show. What is he supposed to be doing?"

"He was supposed to check in with me last week and receive a new assignment. Now that Ross is gone, we need to move on to something else. It is not like him to disappear or initiate something on his own."

"If I run into him, I will let you know. I am on my way to Big Bend and cell service there is spotty at best. You should try that someday."

The conversation ended and Hinton and Fergie were on their way again. By the time they got to Midland, Hinton was tired, and Fergie was restless. Hinton pulled into a truck stop between Midland and Odessa, where he knew they could spend the night. In the morning he could pay five dollars for a shower and have breakfast with the truckers. He took Fergie for a walk around the open area surrounding the truck stop. They both ate and went to sleep in the back of the jeep.

They arrived in Fort Stockton early in the afternoon on Sunday. Hinton bought gas and headed straight to the Parker's house on Third Street. William Parker was sitting on the front porch with their dog Maggie. Fergie knew where they were and was excited to see Maggie. Mr. Parker got up to greet Hinton and said,

"We haven't seen you or Millie in months. Come have a seat. Mary told me she would be out in a minute or two. I'll bet she has some iced tea. The dogs can go run around in the backyard. I am glad they enjoy playing with each other. Maggie needs some time with another four-legged creature. She gets tired of two old folks who don't run very fast. Now tell me what you have been up to and why Millie is not with you."

Hinton described some of what was going on including the death of

Ross, but he left out the details of his recent travels. Hinton did not mention Millie, but William would not let the topic go.

"You know that we think of you and Millie as family. After Billy Joe died, we always hoped that the two of you would get together as a couple. The last time you came here, you brought Millie with you. What's going on?"

Hinton was about to speak when Mary Parker opened the door. She had a big smile on her face and told Hinton to come give her a big hug, which he did. Then she said, "Now young man, where is Millie?"

Hinton explained that he and Millie were still great friends but that anything romantic between them was just not going to happen, but not because he hadn't tried. He told them that Millie had a new love in her life and had made it clear that the two of them would remain friends as they always had been but no more. He told them that Millie's new man was someone they would like, but he was careful not to say who it was.

Both Parkers expressed disappointment and Hinton managed to change the topic. He asked them what they had been up to over the past several months since his last visit. Mary could not resist the opportunity to give William a hard time.

"That youngster over there retired about six months ago. That's not exactly true. He retired for about two days before the folks who run this town convinced him to run for the city council. Worse, the old fool got elected and now he is as busy as ever. Everyone in town needs something fixed – roads, sidewalks, sewers, whatever and now they think he can do it. Someday they will figure out that he is an electrician and not a general repair service. They call him at all hours of the day and night. He loves it. As for me, I still work part-time in the library, which only had about three books when I started. When I am not at the library, I am still the president of the Fort Stockton Women's Coyote Killing Club, but we only kill rattlesnakes, and if that weren't enough to do, I take care of some old fool."

William interjected with a smile, "Mary is almost right. I sold my electrical shop to a young man from Abilene who seems to know what he is doing. I got a good price for it, and I still own the building and two other buildings downtown. You might say I am a landlord. I just sit here and collect the checks. Not a bad living, if I do say so. I kept my electrician's license and still do some small jobs for old friends. I have no idea how a black man who did not want to run for office got himself elected to city council. I let them nominate me, but I did not campaign."

Mary Parker insisted that Hinton stay for dinner and then said, "You know where the spare bedroom is. Go put your stuff in it. You are spending the night."

Hinton did not resist the offer. Mary was a great cook and the thought of a nice bed instead of the back of a jeep was fine with him. Hinton expected fried chicken or a chicken fried steak for dinner, but Mary served salmon filets and a Caesar salad. She said they now limited fried meals to once a month. They felt better and had lost some weight. The three of them talked until late in the night.

The next morning Hinton and Fergie were on the road again. Hinton took his time getting to Marathon where he stopped at the Gage Hotel, a wonderful old place built in the 1920s, designed by the famous architect, Henry Trost. He was not after a room. What he wanted was a chicken-fried steak. The White Buffalo, the restaurant and bar at the Gage, served a chicken-fried steak with jalapeno gravy. Maybe not the best chicken-fried steak in Texas, but the gravy was wonderful. He also ordered a locally famous drink, a prickly-pear margarita. The steak was very good, and Hinton again promised to find the best one in Texas. Hinton had just finished paying the bill when Brinkman called.

"Senator Wilson would like to talk to you. Can you do that now if I set up a video call?"

"Yes. I will get my tablet from the Jeep. Go ahead and set it up."

Hinton retrieved his tablet and used his cell phone as a wifi hotspot. The call came through almost as soon as Hinton was ready.

"OPEC has rescheduled its meeting for next week. I heard your assessment that the Saudis are about ready to announce that they are going green and will reduce oil output by a million barrels a day this year and for each of the next five years. Are they likely to do that next week?"

"No. The Saudis are very sophisticated analysts of energy markets. The markets have been in turmoil for weeks and they are not likely to say anything that will create more volatility. That is not in their best interests or in the best interests of other OPEC members. They will move ahead with their sustainable environment plan, but not next week. My sources tell me that they will maintain output at current levels for a few months and then announce their intentions."

"What about the Russians? Are they going to increase output as the rumor mill, has it?"

"The Russians are much less predictable than the Saudis, but I don't think they will try to upset the OPEC system next week."

"Thank you. Those are my thoughts as well, but the White House is really worried about this meeting given the cancellation of the last one."

"The White House is always worried about what OPEC might do and they are justified in their concerns. That is their job, but they should just calm down and keep quiet until the meeting is over."

"Thanks. I may need to talk to you again soon. You seem to have good sources and some common sense. Enjoy your trip. I have never been to the Big Bend region."

As soon as the conversation with Wilson was over, Hinton looked at

Fergie and said, "We need to go somewhere that does not have cell service."

He said this as if Fergie would understand. They headed south on highway 118 to the park entrance. Hinton stopped at Panther Junction, the park headquarters, and filled up with gas even though he was not close to running out. It is just a good idea to have a full tank in remote areas. Then he headed for Rio Grande Village, near the Rio Grande where he could pick up the river road, a remote part of the park. On the river road you need four-wheeled drive, there is no cell service, and not many people. Just what Hinton was looking for.

For two days, Hinton and Fergie camped near river road and enjoyed the peace and quiet. What Hinton wanted to do next was to have a meal and a beer at José Falcon's in Boquillas, on the Mexican side of the river. Years ago, this would not have been a problem. You simply went to the crossing, paid a guy with a rowboat a few bucks to cross the river – or, if the river was low, you could simply wade across it. There was no customs check and no border patrol. That changed after September 11. There was now an elaborate customs area, you needed to show a passport, and, of course, you could not take your dog. Hinton's only chance, without returning to Fort Stockton and leaving Fergie at the Parkers, was that a former student was now a park ranger at Panther Junction.

Hinton and Fergie took the paved road to Panther Junction. Hinton's student, Robert Travis, was on duty and was happy to see his former professor. Hinton said,

"I have a favor to ask. I need a place for Fergie to stay while I cross the border and have a meal at José Falcon's. Can you help?"

Robert was more than happy to help. He lived in a trailer behind the park headquarters and had a small fenced area where Fergie could stay.

Hinton thanked him and left Fergie, who did not seem to mind.

Hinton filled his gas tank again and headed to Rio Grande Village, a camping area by the river that had showers and a small store. He needed a shower after two days in the boondocks. Boquillas Crossing was not far away. Hinton went through the customs shed, walked the 100 yards or so to the river, paid five dollars for the rowboat. Boquillas is about a mile and a half from the river. You could walk, rent a horse or burro, or get there in a pick-up truck. Hinton had not been on a horse in a while and took that option. The owner of the horse, his guide for the afternoon, went with him.

When he arrived at José Falcon's, he ordered a combination plate and a Mexican beer. The view from the patio was magnificent. The meal was very good and the ice-cold beer was better. It was not quite the same place that it had been before José died, but it was still relaxing. The restaurant and bar had been closed for a year or two after September 11 and again during the Great Recession, but José's wife had managed to open it again and Hinton was happy that she had done so.

Hinton had just finished his meal when his cell phone rang. He had not expected to have any cell service, but maybe atmospheric conditions were just right. He hesitated and then answered. Deuce was on the line.

"I have the same old question. Have you seen or heard from Johnston?"

"No."

"We haven't either. We know that he took a flight from Heathrow to Dulles, but instead of checking in with us, he grabbed another flight to Dallas. There he rented a car. The car was turned in a day or two later at the Oklahoma City Airport. We know he used his keycard to enter the office in Oklahoma City, but he left no messages or other indications of where he might be headed. He has not used his credit cards or accessed his bank account since he arrived in Dallas. Johnston has never done anything like this before. I am beginning to think that he is dead, but no body has been found and we have no other evidence to support this idea. If you hear anything, please let us know."

Hinton promised to do so and then decided to return before the border crossing shut down for the evening. Hinton crossed the border, retrieved his jeep, and headed to Panther Junction to pick up Fergie. They camped that evening in the Rio Grande Village campground. Long before dawn, they headed north to Fort Davis State Park. He had been there many times and always went to the same place. There was a hill at the edge of the campground with a flat rock on the top that could be used as a bench. His memories of that place were intense and comforting. Sitting on the rock with Fergie at his side, he began to think of the young woman who had come to this spot with him. He remembered Kris Kristofferson's song "Loving her was easier than anything I'll ever do again." He often wondered about what might have been, but he knew that he was an incredibly lucky man just to have such a memory.

Hinton's thoughts were interrupted when Fergie who had been sitting quietly at Hinton's feet, growled when the mystery woman sat down beside him on the rock. Before he could say anything, the woman very calmly said,

"Relax, you have nothing to fear from me. If I had wanted to kill you, you would already be dead. You do not need to reach for the pistol in your ankle holster. You do not need to defend yourself in any way."

Stunned, Hinton could only say, "How the hell did you find me? You did not follow me here and I spent two days in the backcountry where I would have seen you."

The mystery woman replied, "The man you call the Rabbi told me where to find you. He told me to be patient, but to look for you near sunrise or sunset at exactly this spot. I have a room at the Indian Lodge, a very relaxing place by the way, for the last three days. I was confident in following the Rabbi's instructions. He has never been wrong before. You brought the Rabbi here once when you were in graduate school. The Rabbi told me that you are not a religious man, but that this place was somehow sacred to you even if that is in a secular sense. If you don't believe me, you can easily check with the Rabbi."

Hinton knew that cell service was limited but he sent a text to the Rabbi anyway. The text was short and to the point: "Rabbi, who is this woman?" If the Rabbi knew her, Hinton was confident he would know who he was talking about. Hinton had several questions for the woman and began to ask them.

"Why are you here?"

"The Rabbi asked me to find you. He did not want you to be looking over your shoulder for the rest of your life. There is no more danger to you."

"What is your name and how do you know the Rabbi."

"My name is not important, but you can call me Sheila. The Rabbi is an old friend. I wish that I had thought of your nickname for Rabbani. It fits him like a glove. We were students at the Sorbonne together many years ago. We were lovers until the Rabbi decided to go off to London to finish his studies at LSE. He was my first lover and I think I was his first. I would do anything for the Rabbi. His wife, Shabazz, is also my good friend and I am happy they found each other."

"Why have you been following me? You were in DC, in London, and other parts of Europe? Now you are here. What are you doing?"

"I followed you half-way around the world because the Rabbi asked me to keep you safe. You were never in danger from me, but you have been in danger since I first started following you near Langley. You really should pick some new friends."

"Did you kill Ross?"

"No. I did not."

"Whoever killed Ross did the world a favor. Ross was a serial killer, not just the mild-mannered professor everyone thought he was."

"Ross did not kill Diane Stoddard, if that is what you are thinking. I know. The evening that she was killed I was following Ross and Cindy Burgess. Ross and Cindy went to Diane's apartment early in the evening. When they left, Diane came out the door with them to see them off. There was another man walking up and down the block where Diane lived that night. I later learned that he was your associate, Chuck Johnston. I left and followed Cindy and Ross, who went to a club near Russell Square. I learned later that Diane had been killed, but I am confident that Johnston did it. In any case, I know that Ross did not kill her. I know exactly where he was that evening and Cindy told me that Ross was a perfect gentleman."

"That fits with other things I know about Ross. I am not so sure you are right about Johnston. Why would Johnston kill Diane Stoddard?"

"Johnston's motive is not important. Maybe he wanted Ross to look like a serial killer. Maybe she knew something about him that could be very embarrassing. I am not certain, but I am confident he did it. The only person who could tell us is dead."

"Why were you following Cindy and Ross?"

"Cindy is my lover. She asked me to follow her that evening because she did not trust Ross but had agreed to go out with him to discuss their mutual interests in the oil and gas industry. They talked about the industry. The club they went to was more than a little strange, but nothing happened between them. Later that evening the Rabbi called me and asked me to keep an eye on you. He told me which hotel you were staying in near Dulles. He was very concerned. At the time, I thought Cindy was safe enough from Ross and I went directly to Heathrow and caught a flight to Dulles. I first saw you in the lobby of the hotel as you were checking in."

"How did you know how to identify me?"

"I never forget a face. Two years ago, at the OPEC meetings in Vienna, the Saudi Embassy threw a big party. The Rabbi invited you, me, and several others. He introduced us and we talked for a minute or two. When he called a couple of weeks ago, I had no trouble picturing you in my mind."

Hinton's phone made the offensive sound that indicated he had a new message. Hinton looked and was surprised that the Rabbi had answered his text so soon. The Rabbi's message simply said: "Trust her. I will explain later."

Hinton had been the Rabbi's friend for more than thirty years. If the Rabbi said he could trust this woman, then he would. Hinton continued,

"Through friends in law enforcement, I learned that Ross had been linked to several other murders in many parts of the world with the bodies all tied in the same way that Patti Walker had been tied. The authorities were reluctant to arrest Ross because they had no fingerprints, DNA, or witnesses to any of the crimes. They have such evidence now. Ross had been a little careless in a murder in Mexico."

"Your friend Chuck Johnston killed Ross. I have no doubts about that. I followed Johnston for two days because I thought he might be a threat to you. I was outside of Ross's condo when Johnston knocked on the door. He only stayed a few minutes and the next day the media had the story that Ross had been killed. I don't know what his motivation was, but I am certain that he did it. I am just as certain that he killed Diane Stoddard."

"A lot of this makes sense now. For Johnston, this was personal, not professional. Johnston had been having an affair, more than an affair really, with Patti Walker. If he was convinced, as I am now, that Ross killed Patti, then this was a revenge killing. By the way, I have had three calls from Johnston's boss in the last several days. He called to find out if I had heard from him or knew where he was. I told him that Johnston had not contacted me since I left London."

"I can solve that little mystery. I killed Johnston and I would do it again. I have no regrets. After Johnston killed Ross, I thought you would be next. I checked with the Rabbi before I did it. We both assume that our conversations are being recorded or listened to. Over the years we have developed a code, almost a secret language, to convey such things. I complained of a stomachache from eating a meal at a friend's house in London and said I never liked the man anyway. The Rabbi said he hoped I got rid of it soon and to let him know when I felt better. Then I did it. Simple as that."

"I think I would have heard if Johnston's body had been found. As far as I know, there are no reports of his death. If you killed him, where is his body?"

"I am a professional. I have done this many times and I know how to dispose of a body so that it will not be found. No one will ever find it. I won't tell you what I did with it. Trade secrets, you know."

Almost in a state of shock, Hinton began to think about what he had just been told. Sheila or whoever she was started to leave and then said,

"I am going to leave now. I don't think you will see me again. With both Ross and Johnston out of the way, you should be as safe as you have ever been. The Rabbi is satisfied with that conclusion. I will walk away and disappear. You will not find me, not even through Cindy. We have agreed that this relationship will not work and that I should not contact her again. You can kill me if you want. You might even get away with it, but I don't think you will kill the Rabbi's friend."

A few minutes later, Hinton called the Rabbi and left a message: "Rabbi, where the hell are you? You owe me a dinner."

Acknowledgments

Marianne Poythress, who got me started on this project and then kept me going, deserves more thanks than I can express here.

Daniel J. Howard, author of *Inside the Front Porch*, read an early version and gave me more useful suggestions than I can count. Thank you Dan.

Richard V. (Rick) Adkisson, Debbie Anderson, Kathy Brook, Garrey Carruthers, Fred Harris, and Lai and Mike Orenduff helped me in many ways. I owe you all a cold one. Many thanks.

Printed in the USA
CPSIA information can be obtained
at www.ICGtesting.com
LVHW020831081123
763364LV00066B/1004